FELL BEASTS

Chris,
Hope you enjoy this anthology of monster tales. Happy Horrors!

[signature]

UPCOMING DARK QUEST BOOKS BY TY SCHWAMBERGER

For After Midnight

UNDER AMBROTOS PRESS
(as editor)

Relics and Remains
Twisted Tales

FELL BEASTS

Edited by
Ty Schwamberger

Dark Quest, LLC
Howell, New Jersey

PUBLISHED BY
Dark Quest, LLC
Neal Levin, Publisher
23 Alec Drive,
Howell, New Jersey 07731
www.darkquestbooks.com

Copyright ©2010, Dark Quest Books
Individual story copyrights held by the authors.

The series name Fell Beasts is a registered trademark of Dark Quest, LLC.

ISBN (trade paper): 978-0-9830993-7-6

All rights reserved. No part of the contents of this book may be reproduced or transmitted in any form or by any means without the written permission of the publisher.

All persons, places, and events in this book are fictitious and any resemblance to actual persons, places, or events is purely coincidental.

Interior Design: Danielle McPhail
http://www.sidhenadaire.com

Cover Art and Design: Thomas A. Erb
http://thomasaerb.webs.com

TABLE OF CONTENTS

SPELUNKING
R. Scott McCoy 1

THE WHISPERS IN THE CAGE
Timothy Moore 9

SAMUEL
Jason Sizemore 25

EXCITABLE BOY
Thomas A. Erb 29

ON FINE FEATHERED WINGS
Gord Rollo 43

IN DARKER WATERS
Robert Ford 51

NIGHT SHIFT AT HOTEL MARA
Dean Harrison 61

SANDWALKERS
Michael West 73

SPLINTERS
Adam P. Lewis 87

THERE GOES THE NEIGHBORHOOD
(Holiday Version/Extended Cutting)
Brady Allen 97

YELLOW
John Everson 113

ACKNOWLEDGEMENTS

I would like to personally thank each and every author that contributed to this anthology. Your stories contain all the elements that make a great collection about creatures, monsters...and BEASTS!

To all the readers I have only one word for you all...beware!

Ty Schwamberger
Editor, Fell Beasts

SPELUNKING

R. Scott McCoy

MARK TOOK A DEEP BREATH, TENSED AND LEAPED ACROSS THE GAP IN THE ROCK. He hung in the air feeling weightless. Free.
His hands grabbed for the handhold, but he'd misjudged. His right wrist cracked hard against the stone as the fingers of his left hand grabbed nothing but air.

He fell fifteen feet before the slack in the rope disappeared and he felt his body pendulum toward the rock. He caught a glimpse of his best friend Phil and belay. He was smiling and shaking his head.

Mark rotated in time to absorb the worst of the impact on with his legs.

"I told you it was too far," said Phil.

"I can do it, just let me rest a bit."

"Forget it," Phil said, "we need to get to the cave mouth before noon. Don't forget why we're here."

Mark hadn't forgotten, but it was hard to pass up a challenge. He'd been in the lead and they were less than fifty feet from the summit when he'd gotten cocky. He'd been making record time and was warmed up, but not the least bit fatigued. The climb wasn't listed in any of the guidebooks and he wanted to make it as challenging as possible.

"Good try," Phil said, slapping him on the back as he passed. From anyone else, Mark might have suspected sarcasm, but not from Phil. He was a great climber and a better friend and Mark was sure he'd wanted him to make it.

"Thanks. No more delays, I'm going to top this sucker."

Mark followed the route and was on the wide ledge in ten minutes. He adjusted his rig and belayed for Phil. Once they were both safely on the ledge, Mark rolled up his rope, while Phil pulled up their packs using a smaller line he'd attached to his harness. Mark tested the wind and once he was confident there was little danger, he dropped his shorts and sent a long yellow stream over the edge.

"Do you have to do that every time we finish a new climb?"

"Hell yes," said Mark. "It's tradition. At least there aren't any kids around."

Phil laughed and nodded his agreement, remembering an unfortunate incident with a group of boy scouts in Yosemite.

"You got that right. There isn't anybody for miles."

After shaking twice, Mark took in a deep breath of Appalachian air. He looked at the cave mouth and the structure of the mountain and hoped he was right about the hidden cavern.

"I sure hope your right about this hidden cavern, Mark. I could be in Myrtle beach this weekend with Pam."

Now it was Mark's turn to smile. "Pam shmam. That woman is nothing but trouble old buddy. Besides, you saw the scans. It has to be here."

"Yeah, I looked at the scans, but I'm a physicist, you're the freakin' Geologist. And Pam is not trouble, she's...interesting."

Mark took a long drink from his canteen and looked at the rock again.

"It's got to be in there. We're going to make a little history today buddy."

They'd dreamed for years about getting their names in a guidebook for being the first to spelunk a virgin cavern. Mark's love of rock climbing had morphed into a degree in Geology. Now, as he wrapped up his PhD, he had access to new satellite technology that was used to monitor fault lines and even search for mineral and oil deposits. Mark had spent months of his spare time going over the scans, looking for an undiscovered cavern. Finally, a month before, he was sure he'd found it deep in the Rocky Mountains of Colorado.

They double checked their gear, put on their miner headlamps and entered the cave. After twenty feet, the chamber angled to the right, starting its downward spiral. They left the sunlight behind, relying on their lamps to guide them. With the elevation and lack of vegetation, Mark expected the cave to be dusty and dry. Instead, there was a faint musty odor. It reminded him of an old litter box.

Phil's beam of light swept the right side of the tunnel and Mark tried to catch a glimpse of at what it uncovered without moving his own beam off of the left wall. They followed the tunnel in silence listening for a tell tale trickle of water or a breeze through a small crack that would give away the location of the cavern.

The tunnel ended at the next turn.

"No way," Mark said, "no fucking way, there has to be more right? You saw the scans?"

Phil nodded.

Mark stepped up to the rock and ran his hands over it. The back wall was unlike the rest of the tunnel. It was about fort feet across and the rock on the left jutted out about two feet.

"Phil, hold your light on this section."

There was a definite crack that was too straight to occur naturally that Mark traced with his finger until it went out of reach overhead. He moved to the right and squatted down, examining the floor of the tunnel. After two minutes, he felt the thrill of discovery.

"Ha! I knew it. This isn't a dead end. It's some kind of stone door. Look, there's a grove warn into the floor."

Phil leaned down and looked, and Mark could see the light bulb go off for him.

"What the heck would something like that be doing here?" Phil asked.

"No clue. Let's find out."

Both men set down their lights and began to push on the edge of the stone door. At first it didn't budge, but after a minute of grunting and shoving with all their strength, the door just rolled away, leaving both men sprawled on the floor. They recovered and shown their lights into the empty space beyond. It was a cavern, about the size of a large college lecture hall.

Before he could think about what he was doing, Mark rushed to the edge of the drop. He'd assumed the shaft would be at least fifty feet based on the data from the scans, but light from a hole in the chambers ceiling revealed at least a hundred feet and there was no sign of the bottom.

Phil peaked over the edge as well, though he was laying flat on the rock and gripping the edge tight. The two friends looked at each other, and then back down the shaft. Without a word, they nodded and started breaking out their gear. Mark took out a light stick, broke the ampoule inside, shook it and dropped it over the side. Both of them watched as the light stick tumbled end over end. Mark was counting and did the math as soon as it hit what appeared to be the bottom. It was close to two hundred and fifty feet, too far to make out any detail from the small amount of light. Phil placed a large cam deep in a crack on the wall opposite the opening, then a second cam in a smaller crack five feet to the left. Mark rolled out the static rappelling rope and waited while Phil tied off nylon straps together and connected a large carabineer, creating a V. Mark Tied a figure eight in the end of his five hundred foot rope and looped it into the carabineer and screwed the gate closed.

Both men still had on their harnesses and both were eager to make the repel.

"Rock, paper, scissors?" Asked Mark.

"No way. You cheat," said Phil.

"You can't cheat. You're just mad because I win more often."

"Try always. No way. Coin toss."

Phil pulled out a quarter. "Heads or tails, Amigo?"

"Tails."

Phil flipped it in the air and both men huddled over the shiny disk, their miner's lights showing the tails side of the quarter.

"Shit," Phil said.

"Don't be a sore loser. We're both getting in the book."

"Sure, but which book?"

Mark thought about it. The Spelunking book for sure, this cavern was a major find, but what about the thing that was at the bottom? It could make them both famous. Maybe even rich.

Phil looked at the shaft walls as far down as his light would go.

"Be careful, the surface isn't smooth and we have no idea what the structure is like."

Mark smiled. "Don't worry, I'll take it easy. Besides, I'm not in a rush. I want to savor this."

He made sure the rope was secured in the metal figure eight that was attached to his harness, slid on his thick leather gloves and started his descent. He walked down at first, letting the ropes slide though his break hand. After five feet, he was confident that the rock was solid. He started kicking out and rappelling ten feet at a time. When he thought he was about half way down, he looked up. Phil was lying down again with just his face and hands showing.

"It looks good. I haven't seen any lose rock or stones. It's jagged in places, but not too sharp."

Phil nodded and gave him a thumbs up and Mark kicked off with more confidence. He took the next hundred feet in three bounds and locked his break hand. He looked down. The shaft remained a consistent fifty feet across and he hadn't seen any side shafts. Since there was some kind of naturally cut chimney in the ceiling, he'd thought the bottom would be covered in sand or water. Instead, it looked like it was covered in jumbled piles of sticks.

Mark let the rope slide through his grip. He descended for twenty more feet and stopped. Less than thirty feet below him was the body of the large fury creature. It was face up and had what he'd thought was a large stick shoved through its stomach. He could see now that they were bones. Fifty feet across and god only knew how deep, the shaft was filled with skeletons. There was some fur visible, but most of the bones were stripped clean.

Mark stared at the grey streaked face. It was no man in a suit. This was Big Foot. Or was it Sasquatch? Were they the same thing? Whatever it was called, the proof that the world had been looking for was impaled on a pile of bones. As he stared into the face of legend, it started to twitch. It looked like it was trying to talk. He knew it wasn't possible. Even without being impaled, nothing could survive such a fall. Mesmerized, Mark let himself slide down another ten feet. It wasn't just the creature's face. The body writhed as if it were in agony. Just as Mark was about to yell up to Phil, the fur ruptured in a dozen places. Maggot white creatures squirted out through the holes and writhed on the top of the body before burrowing back into the meat. They looked like large earthworms, but moved like snakes. In and out they slid as if the flesh was nothing but water, and Marks breakfast exploded downward covering the mouse sized creatures. They swarmed the remnants of eggs and bacon, devouring it in seconds. Once it was gone, they stretched up toward him. Hungry mouths undulating like hairless little birds.

"What do you see?"

Phil's voice broke the spell.

"Pull me up!"

"Are you okay?"

"Pull me the fuck up now!"

There was only a brief hesitation, and Phil started hauling on the rope. Mark pulled himself up the rope as he ascended, not daring to look down. It seemed to take forever, but when Mark reached the top, he scrambled over the edge and rolled a dozen feet away, shivering in disgust.

"What the hell did you see?" Phil asked.

"Buddy, we found the Bigfoot graveyard."

Phil was staring at him, his smile making it clear he was expecting a joke.

"I'm not kidding, buddy, there is a small mountain of skeletons down there and a pretty fresh dead on lying on top."

"You're not kidding. You mean it, I can always tell when your bullshitting me. Shit man, we'll be famous!"

Maybe, but right now we got to get the fuck out of here."

"No way, it's my turn. Let me get down there and see out big footed meal ticket."

"It wasn't alone. There were some things down here feeding on the carcass."

"What kind of things?"

"They looked like some kind of giant maggot. Dozens of them, eating our evidence in record time and last I looked, they were crawling after me. We've got to get out of here."

Mark got to his feet and started walking toward the opening. Disoriented, he looked back at Phil and the rest of the chamber, then back to where the opening should have been. It was gone. He could see the edges of the large boulder that they had walked passed. Somehow, it had rolled closed.

"That can't be," said Phil, "I would have heard it. Wouldn't I?"

Phil joined him and together they pushed with everything they had, but it was no good. The other side had natural handholds, and while he doubted they would have had the strength to move it, it was at least possible. On this side the surface was smooth and they had no leverage.

"It must have rolled back into place. Forget it."

Phil kept pushing, but Mark started searching the rest of the chamber. It was round, with no cracks bigger than his head and about two hundred feet across. He'd hoped that the shaft would lead them to an underground river to explore. He didn't know what was under all those bones, be there was no way in hell he was going back down to find out.

The cavern was getting darker and Mark looked up to the chimney in the center of the ceiling, then back at his watch. Though they'd only been in the chamber for thirty minutes, the sun had been directly overhead before, illuminating it fully. Now, the sun was moving toward the west and the chimney would soon provide minimal light. He'd looked straight up, when he was rappelling and he was sure the chimney less than twenty feet long. It was big enough to climb through. It had to be.

He saw Phil staring and as usual, he came to the same conclusion.

"Okay, but how do we get to it?"

Mark shook his head. The walls had some cracks that spread up to the ceiling, but there was no crack wide enough to wedge their body into. Overhangs took a lot of strength to climb, and this one would be close to fifty feet.

"Listen to me, buddy. We're getting out of here. No fucking way I'm going to be around when those things get to the top."

Phil nodded his agreement. "So what's the plan?"

"We put another cam in the wall opposite the one we got in place and we synch the climbing rope tight. Then we tie our climbing rope to it so if we fall, we fall in the middle of the shaft."

"You think we can make it to that chimney?"

Mark nodded. "You can. You're a better climber than me. It kills me to admit it, but I've seen you hang from a crack a lot smaller than the ones leading to that chimney longer than I could ever hope to."

Phil looked doubtful. He looked over the edge of the shaft and shivered, then looked at the ceiling. Mark watched his friend examine each crack. He was moving his hands and talked to himself like he always did when he was working out a new climbing problem. Mark left him to it and rigged up the second cam. He synched the rope as tight as he could and tied it off. Then he measured out just seventy five feet of climbing rope and tied it off to the suspended line. He worked the rope through his figure eight so he could take up the slack when Phil got closer to the opening so if he did fall, it wouldn't be as far.

Phil tied off the end of the rope onto his carabineer and dipped his hands in his chalk bag and nodded to Mark.

"On belay, climb when ready," Mark said.

"Climbing," answered Phil.

The routine of the ritual calmed them both. Mark marveled as he watched Phil practically levitate up the wall. Phil made the transition from wall to ceiling without pause. The handholds along the crack he was working were just wide enough for a foothold, though Phil chose to swing across the roof like he was on monkey bars for fifteen feet. Then the crack ended and Mark felt a moment of panic.

Phil let go with on hand and dipped it into the chalk bag. He repeated the process with his other hand then swung his feet up and stuck his feet into the crack. He grunted with effort and Mark had no idea what he was going to do next. Phil let go with both hands and hung upside down, attached by a jamming his feet into the crack. He winked. Only Phil. Mark had to smile as he watched his best friend do something that would never even occur to him.

After five swings back and forth, Phil grunted with effort, bent upward and plunged his hands into another crack. He grunted some more then kicked his feet lose and once again, hung from only one hand. He turned his face toward the cavern wall and stuck his feet into what Mark now saw was a wider crack. Three minutes later, Phil had made his way to the chimney and had managed to pull himself into the opening. Once there, he rested, safely wedged in place.

"You are the man!"

Mark couldn't see him, but he knew his friend was smiling.

"Don't you ever forget it either," said Phil. "Okay, Mark. I'm going to climb the hell out of here and put a few cams in along the way. My arms are noodles, so I won't be able to pull you up. Just use the ascenders until you get to the chimney, then your home free. I thought it might be smooth, but this thing is textured. A metal wrung ladder wouldn't easier to climb."

Phil's body blocked the light. Mark heard a slithering sound and whipped his head around to look at the shaft. His miner lamp showed two of the pale white worms undulate over the edge of the rock. They opened their teeth rimmed mouths and little tongues twitched in the air as if they smelled him. They turned toward him and started to crawl.

"Phil! You have to hurry man."

The rope tugged twice in his grip and Mark scrambled to attach his ascenders. He was about to climb when he realized he would have to go to the edge of the shaft passed the things on the floor and suspended himself over the shaft. He dry retched and looked back, his light revealed a dozen of the maggot snakes, all moving toward him. He took a deep breath and ran to his right, praying Phil had tied off the other end of the rope. When he had a clear path to the edge, he leaped and dropped several feet but kept a death grip on the ascenders. He started to swing back and forth in the shaft, coming within inches of the walls. His light showed dozens more of the things, now leaning out toward him, still hungry.

Mark closed his eyes and started to climb until he hit his head on the edge of the chimney. He was far enough into the shaft to get both foot and hand holds and he started to climb. The Chimney was closer to fifty feet than twenty, but Phil had been right about it being an easy climb.

His head broke into the open and he filled his lungs with clear mountain air. The sun hurt his eyes and he closed them tight. After a few deep breaths he opened them and stared up at the deep blue sky. He put his hands on the outside of the opening and pulled himself clear. His right hand landed in a puddle and he wiped a swath of red across his shirt.

"Phil?"

He looked around and saw red everywhere. A coughing noise made him spin around and he looked up into the face of a Bigfoot. It had blood on its mouth a large bone in its hand, fresh meat still clinging to it. The creature let out a howl and dropped what could only be Phil's femur.

Mark screamed and his bladder released, anointing his last ascent. He let go and plunged into the hole. He screamed as he fell, bouncing inside the chimney and cutting his head and hands in a dozen places. Two seconds after he cleared the chimney, he hit the end of his rope inside the crevice. The harness smashed his left testicle into his thigh, cutting off his breath and his scream. He grabbed the rope with both hands and slowed his spin.

He moved his head around, looking for burrowing creatures but the walls were bare. His breathing slowed and he hung there, two hundred feet above the greatest discovery of the Twenty First Century, covered in the blood of his best friend.

The silence was broken by a dry rustling noise above him. He titled his head back and the light revealed one of the creatures as it crawled across the anchor rope. Blood dripped down the chimney onto the knot of his climbing rope. The slug like creature stopped at the bloody knot and began to chew.

ABOUT THE AUTHOR

R. Scott McCoy was born in Kodiak Alaska and raised in Bemidji Minnesota. He currently lives in the northern suburbs of the Twin Cities with his family. He's had over twenty short stories published in a variety of magazines and anthologies.

His 1st Novel, *FEAST*, was released from Shroud Publishing in 2009 and his 2nd novel *The White Faced Bear* was released through Belfire Press in October 2010.

    Scott is the Publisher of Necrotic Tissue, a quarterly horror magazine and is an Affiliate Member of the HWA.

THE WHISPERS IN THE CAGE

Timothy Moore

"Good morning, Jim. Can you hear me? Do you understand?" Dr. Sarah Bray peered into the animal's eyes for any sign of humanity; she jerked back when the beast lunged against the bars. She sighed and scratched a few quick notes on her tablet. "Not today, I see."

The monster roared and thrashed around the massive cage. Sarah winced and covered her ears from the fierce noise. *This isn't working as fast as it should be,* she thought. The brute stalked around its confines, leering at her and grinding its teeth. As it paced around, she scanned for any signs of progress. Under matted fur on its right flank, she spotted a large patch of rough flesh—human flesh. *But it is working!*

※

Medical Log: 10
Subject: James M. Levy
Date: 9/10/2010
Experiment Duration: Day 10

The subject's transformation has been slower than predicted. The metamorphosis is still in stage one, and current estimates put the progress three to six days behind schedule. The subject remains unresponsive to any civilized behavior or intelligent interaction. It only reacts in expected manners consistent with its present animalistic state. Any encounter or interaction leads to aggression and violence.

It is agreed upon by myself, as well as Dr. Julie Benson and Dr. David Hopkins, that because the subject's resistance to the treatment, the dosage of XTM-9A should be increased to 300 units per day to correct the transformation lag. The new increased dosage level will be administered starting tomorrow morning.

"How was your lunch, Jim," Sarah asked.

The beast gazed upon her with torment. Its head and throat quivered and made horrid swallowing sounds. Its voice tried desperately to strain out words that only vanished inside thick growls and barks. This is awful, she thought, staring at the pathetic creature. *How could someone do this to another human being?*

She had been given sparse background information when she agreed to lead the research. Everything involved was *Classified* information. A Defense Department official briefed her that Jim was "a death row inmate, and highly dangerous." She was given a folder containing his criminal record and background. It wasn't pretty.

Sarah smiled at the creature. She always attempted to sound upbeat and encouraging when talking to it. "Your appetite is certainly still there. But you didn't try to eat the tray this time!" The stainless steel pan only had a few tooth holes bitten through at one corner. The previous eight didn't fare so well. "You're improving by the minute."

The monster's left paw had nearly fully reversed into a hand, although its slimy fingers could only form a trembling fist that resembled severe arthritis. Other parts of its body showed signs transition as well. Skin was forming in patches of blistering, red flesh. Hair had stared shedding in sticky clumps days earlier. Still, she had to blink constantly and take mini gasps while near it. The smell was astounding—a horrific blend of wet fur, rotting meat, and something else she could only describe as ammonia. "It won't be much longer," she said.

The shrilling squeal of the rear door hinge pierced out as Julie waltzed in the main lab. "How are we doing today?" she asked the animal. It shifted its attention to her and grumbled out nonsense. "Aww, hopefully your voice will come around in a few more days. You're progressing really well though." It shifted around and rubbed against the steel bars. Fur peeled off and clung to the metal, as jagged claws clanked against the floor.

"He didn't eat the tray today," Julie said.

"Yeah, I noticed that," Sarah said. "He's coming around."

"Good thing...that's the last one. Hey, have you eaten yet? David said he's taking the jeep to get some *local* food. Do you want anything?"

"Oh, local food, huh? What kind of food is *local food*?"

Julie laughed. "I have no idea. But I always like trying new foods, so I told him to pick me up whatever he's having." A comical look of concern draped over her face. "We'll see."

Sarah giggled back. "Good luck. I think I will stick with my salad."

"All right, but you're missing out!" Julie ambled out the main door; her brown hair glittered in the florescent light. She was a wonderful person to have on the team. They really clicked. It made the long, isolated study easy—almost fun—and her veterinary experience was essential until the beast fully transformed.

Aggravating, sloppy licking sounds arose from the cage. Sarah spun back around and witnessed the creature sprawled out on the metal floor licking its one human arm. She winced at the uncouth noise, but tried her best to ignore it. "What's that?" she asked the creature. It completely ignored her.

She crouched down and leaned closer for a better look. A huge scar bulged out just at the transition line from fur to skin. It glowed red, engorged with fresh blood and licked raw. The beast stopped and gazed up at her.

"My goodness," she said. "Where did you get that nasty scar?" The animal stared back at her with an intensity that she hadn't felt since the first few weeks. "Easy boy. I'm not going to hurt you." The beast rumbled out a low, vicious growl, and then commenced soothing its wound. *I should get pictures of that,* she decided. Her stomach gurgled. She checked her watch. *It can wait until after lunch.*

❧

Medical Log: 33
Subject: James M. Levy
Date: 10/3/2010
Experiment Duration: Day 33

Significant progress has been made in the subject's transformation. Human skin has fully formed over nearly sixty percent of his body, with approximately twenty percent in the transition stage. Only the patient's right arm and left flank, wrapping around down the abdomen and extending to the left thigh remain predominantly animal. His human vital signs are approaching normal levels, and so far, the patient's overall health appears to be excellent. It is estimated that the subject will be fully restored back to his human state in eighteen to twenty-two days on the current dosage of XTM-9A.

The patient's speech seems to be fully restored, and his reading and writing skills continue to improve. His aggression levels have also dropped significantly over the past two weeks, as noted in previous log files. It was most notable ten days ago when the patient began regaining speech and was able to communicate with us on a basic level. Monitoring his human vital signs and documenting his emotional response will be the primary focus going forward.

❧

"What's up," David asked. Sarah glanced over her shoulder at the others as she closed the door of their makeshift lounge area.

Julie and David relaxed on the worn leather couch across the way. He threw his feet up on an old wooden chair that was within reach and picked at a stain on his shirt. Sarah and her apprehension wandered over.

She glided a shabby computer chair closer to them, as its worn out wheels screeched to everyone's discomfort. Sarah eased in the chair and began.

"I've been thinking." She paused. "We should tell him about his past. He deserves to know."

"But they told us specifically not to," Julie said.

"I know they said not to, but don't you think he has the right to know who he is? I mean, it's his life, and his past."

David lowered his feet and adjusted to the edge of the couch. "Whoa, whoa, isn't that Classified information? We could get in a lot of trouble."

"They don't care about that. He's going to find out sooner or later anyway."

"Maybe, but that's beyond us. If it finds out its past somewhere down the road that's fine, but I'm not going to prison or jeopardizing my career over some animal."

"He's not an animal! He's a *person*."

"Okay, yeah, it's a person. But is it really worth risking? What's it going to change?"

"It changes everything for him. He has no idea who he is or where he's from, or his family, his friends. His daughter! His file said he has a five-year-old daughter. Don't you think he deserves to know that?"

"Does he?" David said. "He's a murderer! He was on Death Row for crying out loud. He doesn't deserve anything, except the death penalty I guess, according to the courts."

Julie kept her arms crossed in front of her stomach and listened to them. "I don't really see how it would hurt anything," she said. She glanced over at David. "I mean, like you said, it doesn't really change anything, so what would it really matter?"

"Whoa, that's not what I said. I said it doesn't change anything by telling it, so there's no point in risking it. I can't believe you two are seriously considering this."

"Stop calling him *it*," Sarah said. "If you woke up one day and couldn't remember your whole life, couldn't remember your wife and kids, wouldn't you want someone to tell you?"

David darted up out of his seat. "Did it ever occur to you that maybe his daughter and family doesn't *want* him to know? That the Feds don't *want* him to remember? The guy's a murderer and has a history of schizophrenia; it's probably safer for everybody if he doesn't remember anything."

"They don't have the right to decide that! It's his life! I think we should tell him. At least about his family."

"I kind of agree," Julie said. "I would want to know...if I was in his place."

"Well I don't want any part of this," David said. "You two can risk everything you've worked for over some criminal monstrosity, but I'm not."

The intensity in the room softened. Sarah understood his arguments; his points were all valid. "Okay," she said. "That's fine. You don't have to. I'll talk with him this afternoon, privately, so no one else will be involved."

Both women remained seated staring at David. His blood pressure seemed to sink down to regular levels, and the rigidity dissolved from his stance. He nodded back to them and then quietly left the room.

Sarah rose from the awkward chair.

"I think it's the right thing to do," Julie said.

Sarah cast a smile her way. "Me too," she said. "Let's hope so."

Sarah swung open the faded white door into the main lab. Lavender light teetered to life. "Good morning, Jim. How are you feeling today?"

"Hi Sarah. I'm still very sore...and my hand hurts. When do you think it will change?"

She strolled over next to his confines for a better look. Clumps of rough, brown hair littered the cage floor. The powerful musk odor was nearly overwhelming. Jim lay on his back near the bars.

She bowed down and studied his paw. "Well, I see your thumbnail fell off...that's good. It seems to be healing up well. Where's the claw?"

"Back there," he said, pointing to the opposite corner. A seven-inch sickle of bone contrasted sharply off the dark scattered fur. His thumb glowed pink and remained riddled with scabs; the other four fingers were knives swimming in hair. "When will the pain go away?"

She wore her best sympathetic smile and answered him. "Your change is almost complete. I know it must hurt...your bones and skin are adjusting so fast. I would say in another...fifteen or sixteen days you should be *you* again."

"Fifteen or sixteen days?" he repeated. Despair pulled at his face. "I know you've said it's not good, but can't you give me something for the pain?"

Sarah crouched down closer to him and grabbed one of the cage bars. "I'm sorry. I really wish I could give you something, but...with your medicine, I can't. I'm sorry. Can I do anything else to make you more comfortable? I can get you a new towel to cover up with, or some more pillows and blankets." She glanced over his thighs and stomach again as the two regions joined together in mystery behind the white towel wrapped around his waist. "Actually you're changed enough, I could probably get you a pair of David's jeans to wear if you would like."

Jim glanced up at her, and then reexamined his blistery thumb. He carefully wiggled it and then studied his claws as he lightly tapped them against the steel. "Could you stay and talk to me a while," he asked.

"Of course."

Sarah rolled over a computer chair from the table across the room as Jim peeled himself from the floor into a seated position. He gently brushed the edge of his pointer finger claw over the round scar of his arm. He seemed deep in thought when she sat down on the hard seat.

She waited for him.

"Tell me about me, Sarah. What else do you know about me? I can't remember anything."

"Oh, okay. I actually came here to talk with you about that." She stared at him for a moment. He still did not look up at her, not as much as a glance. A talon like milk swept over the scarlet scar—that was his only focus.

"I only know a few things. What do you want to know?"

"Who am I," he said.

Sarah wanted to tell him everything, just blurt it out, but something about the moment, his demeanor or the tone, halted her. She cleared her throat.

"Well, your full name is James Monroe Levy. Um, you lived in Del Mar California, a few hours from here. Um, you—"

"How did I get like this?"

Sarah paused a moment—she knew. "I'm not sure, Jim."

An uncomfortable silence filled the space. He continued picking at the gruesome scar; then finally stopped. He stared into her eyes.

"What else do you know?"

Sarah nibbled on her lower lip as she thought. She swallowed and then answered.

"Well...I know that...you have a little daughter, Jim. Her name is Samantha, and she's five."

His eyes flared to life and he leaned in closer to the bars. "I do? Wh...? I don't remember."

Sarah watched him struggle for thoughts that weren't there. I shouldn't have told him, she thought. She could kick herself. He was on the verge of tears when she spoke to him again.

"Jim, it's alright. Maybe once you're...you're almost healed up. That should help motivate you to get better. You're procedure is almost finished."

He stared off into some distance that she could never reach. "Samantha," he said.

"That's right. I want you to stay positive, Jim, okay? I know it's not great to be stuck in here, but you'll be out before you know it." Sarah checked her watch. "I have to go, but I'll be back later tonight if you want to talk some more okay?"

"Okay."

She rose up and strolled towards the main lab door.

"Sarah?" he said. She stopped and swiveled back around to see him clutching on the front bars. "Thank you."

Jiiiim. Jiiiim. I know you can hear me.

Jim pressed the closed fist of his left hand to his temple, while his right hand wrapped thick claws around his right cheek and scalp. "Shut up!" he said, in a whimpering voice. The nights were long here. He tried to ignore it; he tried to get some sleep, but it hardly worked anymore. Nine hours every night before Sarah and the others came in to check on him. Nothing but your thoughts.

Jiiiim, are you there? The Voice's tone slithered like an asp inside his mind. Its velvety sound drifted in and out of his consciousness without beginning or end.

"Leave me alone," Jim whispered.

Jiiiim, we have to stick together if we want to get out of here.

"I don't want to get out of here."

The voice laughed. *Of course you do. We want to get out of our cage.*

Sweat rolled down his forehead and occasionally spilled over his brow. He snapped his eyes closed and lightly rapped the left side of his head with his fist. He opened his eyes to a sickening sight of hopelessness across the room.

That's right Jim, it's three in the morning...we have another five hours together. We have all the time in the world.

"Please shut up!" He squeezed his eyelids together again and slapped a hand over his mouth.

Shhhhh, whispered the voice, *you'll wake the dead.* It muffled out a laugh that prickled like spiders crawling into his brain. He glanced back up at the digital blue numbers through a prism of tears. Five more hours, he thought. A lifetime.

Medical Log: 43
Subject: James M. Levy
Date: 10/13/2010
Experiment Duration: Day 43

The patient's sleeping habits are getting worse. He is noticeably fatigued, but unable to sleep. The rate of transformation has slowed considerably—possibly due to the lack of rest. I may try talking with the patient at night until he falls asleep. Also, further investigation into the cause of his insomnia will be done.

The room reeked of excrement and sweat when Sarah strolled in for her evening checkup. She blinked a few times and tried to hold her breath without showing it. Poor thing, she thought, but what else can he do? They couldn't risk letting him out yet, so two buckets and a hung sheet partition in the cage was his only bathroom. Flies swarmed in capricious directions all throughout the humid room. Shadows spilled down on his cell where fluorescent lights had fizzed out. She turned on the two oscillating fans before going over.

"How are you feeling this evening," Sarah asked. "Ready for some dinner?"

"Hi, Sarah. Yes, I'm starving."

"Well you're in for a treat because David's on his way back from a food run, and he said it's 'steak night' tonight." Sarah grinned and shrugged. "Hey, as long as *he's* doing the cooking for once I'm happy."

"That sounds great!"

She ambled around to the rear of the cage to exchange clean buckets for the used. Jim lowered his head and scratched at his arm.

"Sarah," he asked. "When can I go outside? I would really like to just walk around for a while and stretch out, and see everything outside. I could help you clean up around here, or maybe help with the cleaning and chores."

Sarah took a little longer than usual returning from bucket duty. She didn't want him to see her face just then. She felt awful.

"I'm sorry, Jim. We can't let you out until you're fully healed. I really wish I could, believe me. I know you've been in there for so long, but I would say three or four more days we can let you out, and maybe set your cot up in the spare office."

She paced back over to him as he sat on floor hunched over, picking at his claws. Hang in there, she thought, it's almost over. "I brought you a clean blanket, too," she said, and fed it through the bars.

"I'm down to three," he said.

"I see that! That's good." She studied the pink patch of blister traveling down the left side of his hip, and disappearing under the pair of boxers David let him have. She gestured toward the sore. "I think just that area and your claws, and then you'll be totally back to normal."

Jim lifted his claws closer to his face at stared deeply at them, rotating them around, checking every angle. "I wish these damn things would just fall off then." He hammered them down on the heavy metal floor; three deep gouges were left sliced into the steel.

Sarah flinched from the noise and her heart quickened. "It's all right. They will soon enough. I mean, look, your pinky nail fell off...when last night, or this morning?

"After breakfast this morning," he replied.

"Well there you go. Just hang in there a few more days. You're doing really great, Jim. I mean that. Can I get you anything else, besides your steak when it's done?"

"Well..." He paused and aimlessly rubbed his hand over the claws. "Sometimes...I hear *voices*." Sarah leaned in closer and focused. "At first it was only at night...but now it comes during the day too." He looked up at her, his intense stare piercing into her eyes like little barbs. "Is that from the medicine? Or somehow left over from when I was a monster?"

Sarah darted her eyes away and dropped a sigh. I can't tell him that, she thought. His daughter was hard enough.

"Well...we're looking into that," she said. "I've asked for some other medicine to be delivered here that might help with that, but it hasn't arrived yet."

Her hands moved with life of their own, trying feebly to gesture sympathy and hope. "Even if it *was* here, though, I don't think we can put you on both at the same time. Once you're fully back to normal I think we can give you the other medicine, and that may help with the voices." Her expression turned as she shuffled even closer to the cell. She paused a moment and then spoke softly. "What do the voices say to you?"

Jim remained seated Indian style on the ground and shook his head. "I don't know. It wants me to do things. It tries to help me get out of this cage." He paused. "I think it's maybe just me wanting to get out of here."

Sarah offered a cautious nod as she nibbled on her lower lip. "Does it ever ask you...or tell you...to do—"

The phone rang. It was only phone in the entire building and Sarah had forgotten about it long ago. It never rang. She darted for the lounge area; it sounded like it was trembling off the hook.

"Hello?" she said. The room went silent.

What do you suppose she's talking about, Jim? That phone never rings.

"Quiet, I'm trying to hear." He pressed his ear in between the cool steel bars and strained a few millimeters closer. She left the door open wide in her rush. After a few silent moments, her voice rose with aggression.

Doesn't sound good for you, Jim.

"Shut up!" he scolded. Muffled tones billowed out from the back room. "I can almost hear it. 'Can't stop?'...'Friday'..." Words glinted through the jumbled tones like fragments of glass. "I can't make it out, but I think it's about me."

They're going to kill you, Jim. They're going to come for you soon.

"No they're not," Jim said. "They're doing all this work helping me. I'm almost back to normal; they wouldn't do that. Sarah wants to help me."

Yesss, Sarah wants to help us, but it's not her decision. Whom do you think is on the other end of that phone? Who is making her so upset? Think Jim.

"I don't know. Could be anything." He readjusted his grip on the bars and clanked his claws through the gap.

We need to get out of this cage, Jim. They're going to kill you.

"Please shut up; I have to think. Just let me think."

We have to stop them, Jim. I just want to help us.

Jim gritted his teeth and clamped down on his eyelids. He tipped his forehead against the dense steel rods, and lightly pounded against them. "Please stop talking to me. Go away." The receiver slammed down with a sharp clap and an echoing chime.

That's not good for you, Jim, said the voice.

"Shut up!" He gazed at the gaping door across the room. Nervousness began eating at his stomach. "Sarah? Is everything all right?" Silence answered back.

That's not good for you.

Sarah stormed down the tight cinderblock hallway to Julie's bedroom. "Hey, where's David at," she asked.

"Um, I don't know. I think he took the jeep a little while ago. Why, what's up?"

Julie snapped her book closed and sat up on the bed. Sarah swung around and shut the door behind her; her cheeks had already set the tone.

"They're going to shut the program down!" Sarah said.

"What? What do you mean shut it down?" Julie's posture tensed. "We're almost finished! And it's working. He's almost fully reversed!"

"I know! That's what I told them." Sarah's arms and hands gesticulated wildly;

her cheeks boiled. "He said the program got leaked and now there's a huge backlash and they want to shut it down immediately."

"What happens to Jim?"

"I don't know. I asked and they just deflected it and said to stop all further tests and dosages, and to gather all the files and research, and be ready to be picked up Friday."

"Friday! This Friday!? That's crazy. We can't have all the data and reports done by tomorrow. What are they going to do? It sounds like they're just want to cover it up, or destroy the records or something."

"Yeah, it does. The colonel was very clear that *all* information be gathered and turned in. I kept telling him that Jim's procedure is nearly done and that it's successful so far, but he didn't seem to care."

Sarah fidgeted back and forth uncontrollably. Her temper flared and rumbled like the lid on a boiling pot. "We have to do *something*," Sarah said. "We can't just leave him part animal."

A concerned expression hung over Julie's face. She rose up from her bed seat. "What did you have in mind? We might not like it, but the Defense Department told us to stand down and stop the research...there's not much we can do."

"Well, I mean he's almost healed. Three or four more days and he should be back to normal again."

"Yeah, maybe, but we don't have three or four days. We have one day." Julie checked her watch. "Actually only about eighteen hours."

"I know, but if we increased his dosages, then these last three shots might be enough to heal him."

Julie sighed and crossed her arms. "I don't know. They told us to stop everything."

"They'll never know we gave him a few more doses."

"What about the side effects? We don't really know what doubling up the shots will do."

"I know that, but if we don't he's going to stay half a monster. It's worth a chance isn't it? Jim wants to be normal again. He's miserable. We have to try it."

Julie's eyes fell to the floor as another sighed escaped. She said nothing for a few moments. "Yeah...I guess we could try it."

"Great! Thank you. I'll start the extra dosage now, and then we can double it for his evening and morning shots. We just won't record anything. Maybe we shou—"

"Calm down," interrupted Julie. "I can give Jim his afternoon shot; you should go lie down a while. When was the last time you got a good night sleep?"

Sarah tried to remember, but nothing really came. "It's been a few nights. I know Jim hasn't been sleeping well, and with trying to catch up on the reports...I don't know, it's all been piling up, I guess."

"Go take a nap and relax a while. Everything will work out. I'll go check Jim in a few minutes and later tonight, too."

"That does sound nice. Are you sure? I feel like there's too much to get done first, and it's too much to pile on you."

Julie laughed. "Don't worry; since Jim turned mostly into a man again, I haven't been doing much around here. It'll be nice to run the check-ups again. I was getting bored."

Sarah smiled back at her. "Okay. Get me up if you need anything."

Julie smiled as Sarah shuffled out the door. "Goodnight."

Julie dashed through the main door, into the lab—into the screams. The hair on the back of her neck flared up as she raced toward the cage.

"Jim! What's wrong!?"

"Help me!" he screamed. "It hurts! Make it stop! Please make it stop!" He lay doubled up on the floor clutching his stomach. Violent coughs erupted from his mouth in between the shrieks. His claws raked across his scalp to brush the hair and sweat away.

"My God Jim, hold on!" Julie sprinted back to the computer desk to grab the cell key, and returned just as fast. She fumbled at the lock. "Where does it hurt?"

"Please hurry! I'll show you."

The heavy padlock snapped open. Julie tore it off the latch and flicked it aside with a moment's thought. She darted inside next to his convulsing body.

"Jim! What's wrong? Show me where it hurts."

Jim's body stopped trembling. He strained his head up to stare into her eyes and tapped a claw against his temple.

"In here," he said. Julie's eyes dilated wide; new screams took over.

Sarah leapt from her drowsy nap to shrieks coursing through the air. She thought she heard Julie screaming, but in her cloudy awareness, the discordance morphed into a man's scream. She listened for a moment. She glanced over at the clock on her nightstand filing cabinet—*6:02...are the Feds are here already!?* The orchid bed sheet sailed across the small space. Sarah sprinted barefoot through the door. The screaming was horrendous.

She raced down the cramped hallway and its chilly concrete floor. The musty smell and dim fluorescent lighting seemed to intensify the panic of the situation.

The screeching vanished halfway there. *Oh God*, she thought, as her mind formed terrible possibilities. She arrived at the hulking steel door moving at full speed. She bumped against it, tugged the door wide open, and darted inside.

Sarah burst inside the darkened room two steps and froze. She screamed until she thought her throat would rupture and her lungs would bleed. Staggering backwards, she slapped against the chilly concrete wall.

All but one of the fluorescent bulbs lay peppered on the floor like a million frosted teeth. The last remaining light swayed violently from its supporting chain, and slung shadows around like tidal waves. The heavy smell of sweat burned into her nostrils. She stared at the open cage resting in the lower section of the room.

Thick streaks of black gore smeared over the floor. David's ripped and sliced body lay contorted in the center of the room; Julie's mangled body jutted out from beneath his, resting in a their collective lake of blood.

"Oh my God," she screamed. She whipped around back to the door; Jim stood in her way.

"Where are you going, Sarah?"

She screamed and darted for the lower level when she felt the sharp claws tear into her shoulder. Her legs collapsed beneath her and she crumbled down the three steps and onto the unforgiving ground.

She winced and wiggled on the grimy floor, rolling from her stomach over to her left side. Her shoulder felt split apart. Blood spilled across her back and around her neck, sliding down her chest.

"I'm sorry Sarah! I didn't mean to hurt you. I was just trying to grab you. I'm sorry!" Sarah cocked her head back toward him to witness him punching himself in the side of the head. "No! I didn't!" he repeated. She managed to get her good arm to the ground and peel herself off the floor, onto her knees.

"Jim, stop! What the hell are you doing?"

"I don't know. I didn't want to hurt them, but...I can't let them take us away." She was almost to her feet when his strong arm slithered around her waist. "Here, let me help you."

"No! Stop!" Sarah screamed. Her left arm feebly pressed away trying to break free, but his arm was iron. "Don't...please!"

"Shhhh," he said, as he gestured one of his massive claws up to his lips. He lowered his voice and pulled her in closer. "I don't want to hurt you, Sarah...I like you. You helped me so much. But *he* doesn't trust you. We have to be careful."

Sarah fed on his every word and her eyes flared wide. He shifted her weight in his powerful arm and she let out a whimper. Fire radiated through her body with every movement.

"Here," Jim said, leading her to the office chair. Five excruciating shuffles and they were there. He eased her into the squeaky chair with surprising tenderness. She shot a glance over to the wall clock. Jim noticed her eyes, and looked back as well. "They're coming for me soon, aren't they?"

"What? No! I don't know." Jim waltzed around the chair and stood behind her. A warm hand touched her wounded shoulder, as heavy, boney daggers draped over the front of her shirt. Sarah couldn't breathe.

"She is?" Jim said. "Are you lying to me, Sarah?"

"What? No!" She felt his hand press, then grind against her slashed flesh. She screamed and squirmed to the side as her eyes clamped shut and pressed out tears. "Jim, *stoooop!* Please!"

"Tell us the truth."

He eased up and let the weight of the thick claws brush over her right breast.

He grazed them up her chest and gradually let the point dig in.

"Nooo! God, Jim, Stop it! Please! Yes, they're coming tomorrow! They'll be here in the morning!"

The jagged ends like milky thorns halted their advance. He leaned over her and steered his head next to hers as she darted her face away. His hot breath tasted like smoke and rancid meat. It steamed against her throbbing neck with every breath. She clutched the sides of her seat and tried not to tremble as the whispers swarmed her ear.

"Thank you for the truth," he said. "I like you, Sarah. You've always been so nice to me." He paused. "Mmm Hmm," he mumbled, letting the three talons trace back down over her breast. Sarah shivered and flinched away as a claw tip grazed over her nipple. More tears rushed up as she felt the situation turn.

"That would be nice," he said. She felt him lean further over the chair and stare down her bloody tee shirt, to the hint of bare cleavage beneath. Hot air stormed from his nostrils upon her skin. Sarah's focus sank down to the low-cut sleep shorts she had been napping in. She grasped the sides and tried to tug them for a few more inches of coverage as a tear plopped down upon the pink fabric and formed a vivid wet dot.

"Yeah," Jim said. Sarah began to cry without control. Horrific images of rape flickered through her imagination. She glanced over at the gory corpses decorating the floor, and she squeezed her eyes shut. She could almost hear the sinister voice in his head, leading him, guiding him toward horrifying sins.

The claws like fat ice cycles glided over her breast and slid down to her stomach. Sweat seeped from her shuddering body, and his panting condensed to a film of wetness that trickled down her back. His other hand found excitement by gliding through her hair; his scabby fingers emerging and sinking again like dolphins playing in the sea.

"Please don't do this," she begged. She thrashed her head away until Jim clutched a handful of gold. He slipped one thick claw between her thighs, caressing up and down over the faded cotton. He towed her face closer for a kiss on her cheek, then to a pair of terrified lips. She wanted her hatred to flow through him and ignite him on fire; she wanted his hands and nasty, violating mouth to roast and burn until nothing remained.

"Mmmm, she does," he whispered out.

Her breathing accelerated into gasps, then to wheezing. Pleas escaped her, blended with indistinguishable, helpless moans. "Pleeeease! Stop!" She squeezed her thighs together, but the talon continued to rub and knead against her shorts, and against her sensitive flesh. He fought to keep her head still as the kisses intensified. Saliva smeared across her chin and cheeks, down over her neck—wherever his frantic mouth darted. He scraped his rouge tongue down her neck again and sucked hard against collar, twisting over top her to kiss her chest.

Sarah's fear had lasted long enough. A rage sparked to life and coursed like lava in her veins. Her thrashing snarled to a new plane of violence, and the sharp twinges from pulled hair only fanned her fire. He tried to pull her face to his once more as she ripped away and screamed—screamed louder than she could ever remember.

"Get the fuck off me you monster!"

She felt his coarse fingers detach from her cheek instantly, and his lusting claw jolted from her thighs as though they were electricity. Sarah's heart pumped wildly and she huffed breaths through her mouth.

"Oh my God! Sarah! I'm sorry, I'm sorry!" Jim lunged around the chair to face her and smacked his knees down to the floor. He rested eye level with her. "Sarah, I'm sorry! I didn't know what I was doing. The Voice told me it—"

"Get the fuck away from me!"

"Sarah, please, I'm sorry. It's the *Voice*." His apology carried him forward, closer to her. He rested his hands on her knees without realizing, but then jerked back as though he had touched a scalding pot.

She thrust her foot out to kick him, but he clamped around her ankle and darted in just a few inches from her face. His lean, muscled physique gave hints of its weight against her thighs and chest. A claw point dimpled the pulsing skin of her throat. Fear was in charge once more.

"I don't want to hurt you, but I can't control it anymore, Sarah. It's telling me you're going to kill me if you get the chance." He mashed his eyelids together and shook his head violently from side to side. "It's not her fault!" Tears traced down over his oily cheeks.

"Jim. Jim! Look at me. Don't listen to the voices; listen to me. Focus!"

His eyes stayed shut, but the shaking morphed into nodding.

"Jim, I'm not going to hurt you. Just let me go."

She stared at him, and then glanced at her surroundings. The chair was an island; nothing was useful to her from here. Her senses and thoughts had cleared enough now though. She could smell the salty sweat leaking from his body. She felt the warmth throbbing out from his face and the tiny quavers in his body from shaking muscles. Shrill chirps escaped the worn casters whenever he shifted. Her eyes widened when she felt his weight gradually ease onto her body even more.

His eyes remained closed, but calmer, and the tears ran dry. The white tusk relaxed against her neck and tickled down her collar to the delicate edge of her cotton shirt. She felt the heat pour from his nostrils onto her chest, and the heat from his hips radiate between her legs.

In a nervous whimper, she tried to reconnect. "Jim? Jim, don't do this. Listen to *me!* You're a good man...don't listen to them."

He hoisted his body up and away from hers and screamed. Mercilessly, he beat his fist against his forehead. "It won't stop." He swung back toward her. "You're not safe here. I can't trust myself, Sarah. I don't want to hurt you." His eyes turned away and his teeth clamped tight. "I don't! No!"

"Jim, please let me go. Help me."

He shook his head. "It's not safe around me. You have to be safe." He shot a glance across the lab and stared. Sarah turned the same direction to see the front edge of the cage reaching out from the darkness.

"Stop it!" said Jim, as he smacked his palm against his forehead twice. "We have to hurry. Here."

"Jim, wai—"

He scooped her up into his arms. Her shoulder stung and throbbed, but not as much as she anticipated. He lifted her as though she was an infant, and carried her over the blood and bodies and broken glass with urgency, but with tenderness she never expected.

He eased her bare feet onto the chilly cage floor and stepped back. "I'm sorry for this, but I have to keep you safe. Please understand."

Sarah nodded, but stared at the floor holding her wounded shoulder.

He swung the hulking steel door closed, picked up the shiny pad lock from the floor, and snapped it shut on the latch. "Do you have the keys?" he asked.

Her right hand reached for her pocket only to feel her pocket-less sleep shorts. "No, I don't have them."

"Okay. I'm sorry for this, Sarah, but now you're safe, and they'll be here in a few hours and let you out." Jim gestured toward the murky rear bars with his human hand. "There's water and my lunch that I didn't eat back there." Sarah nodded at him with her eyes lowered, but didn't turn to look.

"No!" Jim yelled.

Sarah jerked away from the bars, eyes wide and startled. "What," she asked.

He gazed at her with a deeply apologetic face. Tears leaked out from his reddened eyes. "No, no, not you. I'm sorry." He fell against the bars and gripped them tight. Two of his three claws penetrated through the gaps by default, clanging and knocking and resembling walrus tusks chewing through the bars. Jim crouched down and squished his face partly between two bars.

"You don't know what it's like, Sarah. You don't know what it's like inside." Jim ripped his nails out from the bars. He stabbed the point of a claw to his temple and violently scratched slices into head. "It never sleeps! It never stops!"

The motor shut off once the jeep parked on the inclined concrete drive. The citrine sun burned through the freckled sky. Jim stayed in the driver's seat and stared at the house, observing all of its features as the engine ticked.

Good work, Jim. We're home.

"What if she doesn't want to see me," he asked. He spread the manila folder open on the passenger seat and sifted through the messy pages until he found the sheet. A picture of his ex-wife remained paper clipped to the upper corner; her current address and brief biography read to him through Courier font. He doubled checked the listed address number with the digits fastened to the porch.

Of course she wants to see you, Jim. And your daughter does too.

"I've never seen my daughter." He scratched a claw beneath his daughter's name on the page—*Samantha Dawson*. "She doesn't even have my last name."

That's alright. That's her mother's name; it's alright. We're home now, Jim. Now we can see her.

He lifted his gaze back to the house and noticed that a woman stood at the door, peering out from behind the ornate glass. "It's Amanda," he said.

Yeeessss. She hasn't changed much since we last saw her, has she, Jim? She looks as young as ever. Let's go say hello.

"She'll be terrified of me," he said, as he glanced down at his claws.

She will understand. Don't you want to see your daughter? We deserve to see her, Jim. She is ours.

He looked back to Amanda standing in the entryway. She seemed nervous now. Her brown hair swayed with every movement as she shifted and strained to see.

"You're right. She is *my* daughter; I have a right to see her. I can't believe she's already five."

Exactly. She is our daughter. Let's go see her. Amanda can't stop us.

The jeep door popped open. "What if she doesn't let us see her?"

The voice paused a moment as he climbed out onto the driveway. *Then we will do what we have to do, Jim.*

ABOUT THE AUTHOR:

Timothy Moore graduated from the University of Louisville with a BS in Mechanical Engineering, and from Auburn University with an MS in Mechanical Engineering. Aside from writing short stories, he is currently finishing his first novel. When not writing, he spends his time reading, playing guitar, acquiring a blend of useful and useless facts, and fumbling around the craft of woodworking. He lives in Ohio.

SAMUEL

Jason Sizemore

You can go crazy waiting for your mother to die.

The purple ringlets circling his eyes told the whole story. He'd been by her bedside for two weeks, most of that without sleep, food, or shower. Family members offered him succor. "Please, Samuel, come eat and have a nap. Your brothers will sit for you." The pleas went unheeded. He remained on the floor, kneeling, holding Mother's left hand in his, willing his life force into hers, across the physical confines of their bodies.

Mother suffered from an acute respiratory ailment, something that mystified all the doctors and all the specialists, and one after another shrugged to Samuel and the family, eventually leaving her to die. Those not offering hope or a cure, peddled their opiates, promising her a restful respite into the arms of death. One had wanted permission to study Mother, her lesions and poor breathing, to put her case in the journals so that "she might save others." Samuel had said "No." And now Mother clung to the fading tethers of life, nearly all important bodily functions aided by machines, the world's technology holding back eternal darkness.

Then, at the quietest hour of another despairing night, while the house and animals slept, Samuel heard a sharp knock on the door. Having no sense of time, he wondered. *Could this be another uncaring doctor, promising miracles if we allow Mother to be lab rat?* He swallowed the stomach acid burning his throat. The knock went unanswered, unwanted.

Yet, the door creaked open.

And instead of the familiar sound of his brother's dirty field boots clacking against the dusty wooden floor, or the graceful shuffling of his sister's feet making a night call to the bathroom, Samuel heard a pitter-patter, like the sound of a rat skittering across the kitchen floor under the cover of darkness.

His heart quickened. This was no rat. He knew who was calling.

"You are not invited, leave this house," Samuel said, his voice disrupting the silence like a stone dropping into a pond.

The little devil walked around the bed, and at first, only the tip of its little orange tail showed above the line of the bed, bouncing up and down as the beast walked. Then it appeared in front of Samuel, standing and smirking.

And then the devil spoke. "Only the call of death invites me. And your business here is over."

Samuel looked upon the thing. The only clothing it wore was a hand-sewn loincloth, the color and texture of dried human skin. Its little fingers moved incessantly, like a jittery pianist over the keys of a grand piano. Black beady eyes were embedded in an oblong head the color of a ripe, red apple. Tied to hemp cord around the devil's waist was a box made from polished camel bone.

"Heed thy words, devil. Your works are not welcomed into this household." Samuel said.

The tiny devil smiled. "Hush your nonsense, pathetic human, and hear me now. I am alpha and omega. My eyes have witnessed the transcendence of time from creation past to the death of your dear, *sweet* old mother. Save her from the pain that feeds on her body and release her soul unto me. For not until then will she have peace."

Samuel stood quickly. "You speak lies, devil. Why should I not stand and crush your impetuousness with the flat of my foot?"

The room lurched from side to side, the walls melting away to expose a great landscape of dying creatures. Samuel witnessed his childhood pet dog, Buddy, howling into the abyss. Buddy then whimpered, and his flesh transformed to the raging hunger of a million black flies. There, in a dead ash tree with limbs fingering upward into the hellish crimson sky, Uncle William twisted from a knot of rope, hanging by his neck, gasping for air. On an elevated pile of holy marble, a fetid pool of maroon fluid bubbled and boiled as an undeveloped fetus cooked in the heat, the remains of the miscarriage Samuel's wife had two years earlier. The visions sickened him, weakened his resolve, but he remained resolute.

A blast of heat melted the skin from Samuel's body, forcing a cry of horror from his mouth. The little devil morphed into a beast with the hooves of a goat and the body of a giant with six arms. Fangs extended from the giant's gums as it drew close to the trembling man.

"What say you now, human?"

Samuel looked down and watched his heart beating inside the cavity of his chest. Blood oozed from the exposed musculature of his forehead, coating both eyes and drowning his vision in a sea of red. He trembled, and feared losing his sanity, but his left hand still held firm to his mother's. Connected. Still alive.

The world shimmered and Samuel rejoiced when the visions disappeared. His eyes widened as the flesh grew back on his body.

The tiny devil remained next to him, smiling.

"She is ready," said the devil.

And then they both were quiet.

Samuel stayed by his mother's side, holding to her hand. The devil stood in place and continued smiling. Time passed, but Samuel would not move. His belly cramped and the burning acids of his stomach belched out of his mouth. The sun traveled its eternal path three times over, yet no one came through the bedroom door to aid him in his stand against the Prince of Death.

On the fourth day, Samuel's mouth became so parched that his tongue cracked and blood flowed down his throat. The taste of fluids delighted his senses. He swallowed greedily of his menstruations.

"Sinner, taste your blood and be sated," said the devil.

By day six, Samuel's bowels released forth a gush of relief and embarrassment that tainted his body and the floor. The death devil laughed and summoned a swarm of green flies to make feast.

Day seven arrived. Samuel heard the sound of thunder outside and rain pounding on the roof of Mother's house. The devil stopped smiling. Mother groaned.

"I have an eternity to spend on my whims," the devil said. "But I tire of your games, human."

"Then let my mother continue to live. Return to your hell and leave us be."

"Cosmic chance did not bring me here. I am here because of your spiritual beliefs. You, her, humanity, all have tilled the ground in which you will be buried. Your mother's soul will be culled, to be claimed by its rightful owner."

Samuel, now a ghost of a man, shook his head. "I love my mother. She stays with me."

"Perchance you should suffer as she suffers?" asked the devil.

Samuel scowled. "What suffering is worse than the death you offer?"

A blinding light enveloped the bedroom, and when the after images in his eyes disappeared, unbearable pains began eating into his body. Each breath squeezed tears from his eyes. A pulsing soundtrack of agony hammered into his soul and the bedroom contracted and expanded to the beating of his heart. Samuel cried out for mercy from the death devil.

"This is how your mother lives. I ask you, this is better than death?"

"No!"

"Are you prepared to release her to me?"

Samuel released his mother's hand and fell to his hands and knees, onto his puddle of excrement, sending the green flies into flight. "Yes, take her, goddamn you, take her," he whispered, the torment and anguish rendering him immobile. A second later, all the machines that kept Mother alive sparked, short-circuited, blanketing the bedroom with the sour odor of burnt ozone and scorched electronics. The death devil raised his arm and fist, as if in victory, and held skyward the camel bone box.

"ταΐζω the παράδεισος με αυτήν ψυχή."

Then old Mother took a last breath and died.

The devil snapped the box shut.

Samuel cried, not for his mother, but for himself. With her death, the torment did not subside.

"You are to suffer four and twenty days for meddling in my affairs. Pray that you have the strength to endure, or I shall be back and your pain will be unmatched in human experience."

The death devil attached the box to the hemp cord. He stared at the human for a brief moment, before walking around the bed, opening the door, and walking out.

"Samuel, are you alright?" It was his brother. "What has happened to you?"
"I have lost," Samuel whispered. "I have lost."

ABOUT THE AUTHOR

Jason Sizemore is the award-nominated editor of *Aegri Somnia, Gratia Placenti, Dark Futures* (Dark Quest Books) and *Apexology: Horror*. For five years he was the fiction editor of *Apex Magazine*, a professional-level online zine of dark SF and fantasy. Since 2004, he has own and operated Apex Publications. You can find him online at www.jason-sizemore.com.

EXCITABLE BOY

Thomas A. Erb

.

MAMA, I HATE THIS PLACE. IT SMELLS LIKE ROTTING FISH AND MOLD. I DON'T mind the dark too much. It makes me feel safe—just like when you used to wrap me in the scratchy orange blanket and rock me back and forth really fast. The sun hurts my eyes so I don't go out much when it's high up in the sky. I like the nighttime. It's comfy and makes me happy—just like that blanket you gave me Mama. I still have it with me. I never put it down—'cept now I made it into a hood to keep my head warm and safe from all the flies and other nasty bugs that live in this movie place with me. I also wear it in case I do have to go outside during the sunny time. It doesn't help that good, but it's okay; I think of the cool, dark basement and it make those times go fast.

Nobody can find me down there. No sir.

What's that Mama? Oh, the puppet? Yeah, I know you told me to throw it away but, besides you, it's my only friend. And I like his little brown cowboy boots and neckerchief. I don't know who Howdy Doody is, that's what you call him, right Mama? I like how he dances, with this little arms and legs bouncing all around. But he is really nice and talks to me when you're away and I'm alone. He's funny and he gives me some really nifty ideas. Ooops, he told me not to tell ya Mama, I'm sorry. A boy has to have some secrets, don't he?

"I'm sorry Mama, no more secrets, I promise. Yeah, pinky swear."

Dang it! There they go again! I just want to be left alone. Why do they keep bothering me Mama? I just want to be left alone!

My arms and legs hurt. I've been cramped up in this cobweb-filled movie picture room and I really need to stretch my legs. But if I go out, they will be there, screaming and crying and I will have make them be quiet. Their sounds hurt my head. It feels like two big rocks squishing my brains together. It hurts and makes me cry and that makes me mad. When I get mad, I just...just feel all whooshy. I want to punch and kick anything to make the noises go away. I never want to hurt nobody. It hurts my heart to make them leak. I cry and ask them to stop. But they never listen Mama.

I used to come to this movie place when I was a kid. Used to eat popcorn by the buckets and guzzle soda pop by the gallons. It was the only place in the whole wide world wheres I felt to home. It musta been the dark. Yeah, I like the dark. Did

I tell you that already? Sorry, Mama said I talk too much and say the same thing a bazillion times. Sorry.

Yeah, they called it the Clerk, or Clark, I dunno. I don't remember too good no how. But it was my favorite place when I was a kid. Well, heck now too I suppose. Can't recall how old I am. I'm guessing twenty maybe; don't really care neither. Guess it don't matter. Do you remember Mama, when you used make me big white cakes with sparkling big white number candles on 'em? I loved it when you would buy those trick ones, where they never go out. I used to laugh until my sides hurt and you would wipe my tears away.

Shush! You... you hear that? Yeah, those high school kids are back! Let's go down to the storage room, we should be okay there.

I have learned how to get from one place to another in this part of town but still only like to stay here in the movie place. Mama taught me good. Right Mama?

I can't stand the loud noises those kids make. Can you hear it? Sounds like that evil loud rock and roll music. I hate that stuff. Oh, sorry Mama, I didn't mean to curse. It's just that they all those mean and rowdy kids come here to drink their beer, do the nasty sex stuff or chase stupid ghost. Why can't they leave us alone? Daytime is okay, it's quiet and I can sleep, but now it's nighttime again and they'll never leave me alone. No Mama, I don't want you to go anywhere! I need you.

Watch your step Mama, the floor is slipper here. Oh, it's just another one of my puppets, her name is Ginger. Don't worry, she won't bother you. It's where she leaked when she wouldn't stop yelling at me and calling me mean names. But she's sleeping black now. She hasn't made a noise in a long time. She' starting to stink really bad so follow me to the back room.

Whoa, look out Mama! I forgot about her. It is slippery in this hallway. Patti's been napping here longer than Christi has, the nasty flies don't seem to bother her any. She looks so peaceful. I think she needed a long nap. Come on, follow me. Yeah, Howdy don't like her much either, but he just keeps telling me I'll get used to it, so I listen.

I know...I know Mama. I don't know why you hate him so much. He's my bestest friend and he keeps my brain even-steven. And I know he tells me to do some mean things sometimes, but it's usually when you are sleeping and I don't wanna bother you, so since he's my bestest buddy, he knows best. Right? Oh, don't look at me like that Mama, you know it makes me cry when you look so sad. Oh darn it, those kids are back; let's head down that hallway to your left. They don't know about that one. There, we can be alone.

What's up those stairs right there? Oh, that's the kiddy section. Yup, that's where the little ones go to watch all those really funny cartoons. Ya know, Scooby Doo and Thunder Cats. Them's my favorites Mama. I know you remember. But don't worry about up there Mama, nothin' to see. Come on let's keep going. Watch your tootsies.

I didn't like being alone in the beginning. The darkness scared me. I don't like the creepy crawly things that share the black spots that I do. I still haven't gotten used to them. The spiders are the worst. I know they don't mean to be scary, but I think about them and I feel them crawling all over me and it makes me shiver and feel all ooggie.

I know, I know! Sssh.

I hear him too. He's calling for Sherri...I don't know her. Maybe she's lost....maybe I could help her find her way home.

She won't hurt me Mama! Why do you always say that the girls will hurt me or make me cry? I never have a chance because you think they all are dirty girls, tramps and whores who just want to show me their fishy parts?

Oh, shush, someone is coming!

I can hear her breathing. She sounds like she's been running. I think she's crying. She keeps calling out for God to help her. Mama, she needs me. There might be someone out there hurting her.

You stay here just in case. I'll be right back. I promise.

Yes Mama, of course, pinky swear.

I know Mr. Howdy, I know, but I feel bad, but being away from Mama for a while, makes me happy. I love her more than Capt. Crunch and my Rubix Cube, but she squeezes me to tight. I need to get away. And besides, I think that Alexis-Baby needs my help. I know the way through the dark movie place good. I will just follow her crying. I hear other kids too, but I speed up, hoping to find Alexis-Baby before they do! I don't want anything bad happen to her. She has said really, super nice things about me. She thinks I'm handsome. Mama don't think I am. Nope, she says I look like Daddy. I ain't ever seen him so I don't know. But, Alexis-Baby has beautiful white skin. Like when the snow comes down from the sky. It looks clean and fresh and makes my pants grow when I think of her. Mama says when my pants grow that I'm making God mad. I feel bad but it happens all the time. Especially when I make the girls sleep black. I know it must be wrong, but my willy grows and I want to do bad things. The bad thoughts fill my head all up and it hurts so much and won't go away until I do what they tell me. Oh, you understand, don't you Mr. Howdy! It makes me smile and feel better knowing that you do. We won't tell Mama okay. Yeah, high five!

But we need to find Alexis-Baby-Baby. She needs me. She and her jerk head boyfriend have been coming here for a few weeks now, with their mean friends. I guess they must be from the school place down the road. I wanted to go to school but Mama says they teach Satan's word there and that they're all sinners and someday, God's gonna come down and turn them all to salt. I dunno what she means, but Mama is always right. We gotta a college a few miles out of town too, but I ain't never been that far out. It don't make no matter, because heck, the whole basement is full of them college kids chasing ghosts and bad things. I don't know why they keep coming in here. There ain't nothin' but me and Mama here, well us and the all the sleeping black people. But they don't know about them and I just wish they would just leave us all alone.

Oh, you think so too Mr. Howdy? Thank you very much.

I hear them. I think they are in the main theater. Shush. Stop talking Mr. Howdy! Hear 'em? Me too! That boy, Alexis-Baby's boyfriend Tony. I think that's his name. She would call his name a lot when they go up to the other balcony and make dirty on the floor up there. She cries, screams his name and asks God for help too. He is a mean boy and needs to be punished, like Mama does, when I'm bad. When I find him Mr. Howdy, I will be him leak and I will like it. I might even get a willy.

You like that? You are laughing and it makes me giggle. Shush, we need to be quiet as a church Mr. Howdy. They will hear us.

If you look through the peephole here that I made, you can see what those mean kids are doing in my movie home.

Ah, I can't see anything either Mr. Howdy, They must be down by the stage. I can hear 'em, let's head down that way and I know a good spot to check em' out from above. The way is dark so hang on tight. I know, I know, I have a hold of you by the strings, but still. You never know what those jerks may have put in our way. Or worse, those icky spiders might have made their sticky, icky webs across the hallways, like they always do. It makes me wiggle and want to shake right out of my skin just thinking about all those little legs running all over my body.

Oh, don't worry Mr. Howdy, I'll protect you. It's not that far and I can see really good in the dark so we will be good.

Ohh, uugghhh, umpfff.

Damnit!

That hurt so bad. You okay Mr. Howdy? I didn't mean to drop you. I forgot all about Robin, Ellen and Stacy. I put them here a long while ago. I hope you're okay? I forgot all about them girls. It got so full in the basement and attic; I had to let them sleep here. Plus, goodness gracious, they never stopped yakking it up. These girls just kept talking, my head hurt, and Mama got mad at them and made me move them. Here, let me ungooble your strings.

I'm really sorry Mr. Howdy, I really am. We better get movin' I hear Alexis-Baby crying again and that jerky Tony shouting bad things and using curse words. The stage is right ahead, right next to those big red, cushy curtains.

Oh, goodness, I hear him. He's—

I didn't want to hurt him. He scared me. His eyes are so wide. I can't let him scream. I grab him by the neck and tug him close to me. Mr. Howdy, tell me what to do! Please!

My hand finds the handle of the big knife easy like from the leather holder on my hip. I don't mean to stick him with it. He just scared me is all. His blood feels warm on my skin. It feels good—it's really cold here. I can hear him trying to say something. It's best if I keep it quiet. I need to get to Alexis-Baby. I don't wanna be surprised by more of her stupid friends.

Oh shoot! I hate it when my hands get all gooey and sticky from the red stuff. I will let him lie down and let him sleep. I hope he doesn't sleep black, but he scared me. I'm sorry mister; I didn't mean to hurt you. Sleep tight, dream big mister.

Stop laughing Mr. Howdy! It's not funny—oh God, someone else coming!

They... she is calling out for somebody. I can see lights from the theater shining in here, backstage. I don't like the yellow. It sees me too much.

Come on Mr. Howdy, there's a place behind the big screen where we can hide and get a goodly look for Alexis-Baby. Oh, no I won't hurt her! Why do you always tell me to hurt them? Haven't I gave you enough of them? Goodness gracious Mr. Howdy, how many do you need?

I'm sorry. I'm sorry. You are right! Please forgive me.

Let's get closer. I can hear them, can you? Yeah I know. They are saying some really mean things about me and my Mama. I don't like that one little bit. Uh uh, no way today.

Hold on Mr. Howdy, while I put you in your pouch on my back.

Ah, there ya are. Are you all comfy-caboodle back there? Can you see okay?

Cool beans. Now, let's go find Alexis-Baby and her mean ol' boyfriend. He makes me mad and I think he needs a stern talkin' to.

※

"Hey sweetie, do you think Howdy Doody Monster is gonna come get ya?" Alexis teased and tweaked her nipples through her tight white, wife-beater shirt. Her smile was meant to tease and arouse her nervous boyfriend, who hung back, close to the door that led back to the lobby of the rundown Clark Theatre.

"Ah man, come on now Sherri, you know this place bugs me out," Tony pleaded grabbing the rusted and cobwebbed handle of the worn door. Not much light was allowed to break the blackness of the large, old theater. The soft beams from their flashlights made little impact on the thickness of the Clark.

"Hey, where did Eric and Lindsay go?" His voice croaked. He wanted it to come out more manly, but as always; it never worked that way for him.

"Where do you think they went silly?" She was almost to the inch thick covered intricately carved wooden stage. "I'm guessing they're having some booty time."

The small shafts of light from their flashlights danced and bounced about the long-condemned movie theater. Not nearly enough illumination to make Tony feel safe, as he finally caved in and cautiously made his way down the dust and grime incrusted red carpet that lead down the aisle to his waiting hottie girlfriend.

"What the hell is that smell?" Tony crinkled his long nose as he sniffed the stale air. Something smelled—dead.

"Ooooohhhh, it must be the rotting bodies of those skank bitches from school that Howdy Doody has stacked up around here smooches." Her large blue eyes seem like a beacon in the desolate theater—drawing him down to her, like a black widow would welcome her doomed lover. He was creeped out for sure, but the growing member in his jeans had other plans. And Lord knows he was never one to think with the big head.

The old theater was a haven for the homeless and partying teens for years. The last film that was shown on its tattered and yellowed screen was Return of the Jedi. The rundown Vaudeville Palace was once a thriving center for the small town of Sterling Point. But, now, it was a puss-oozing, eye sore that the town planning committee had slated for demolition for the past ten years. But the delinquent son of the mayor owned it and was content with just letting the decrepit building sit and rot. Rot like the multitude of corpses that lay festering and rotting inside the dust covered, red carpeted walls.

"Eh babe, you getting scared? You hear that? I bet he's hiding somewhere in here. Or better yet..." Her wide blue eyes feigned horror as she whipped her head around, looking in all directions. Her tone was mocking him, but he was used to it.

"Knock that shit off," Tony huffed, shaking his head.

"What's wrong? You think that Eric and Linds are all strong up like meat puppets backstage? Huh, do ya babe? She bent over the old dust crusted seat, exposing her ample cleavage and gave them a slight jiggle and smiled.

"Ooooohhhh. The big Howdy Doody man is gonna snatch you up and gut you like a deer...dear?" Her laughter filled the large room. It sounded hollow and empty.

"Shut the fuck up," Tony teased as he grabbed her in his arms and smacked her ass. The fleshy slap echoed of the cobweb covered walls.

"You are such a big pussy." She winked and blew him a kiss.

"Keep talking shit and I'll do more than smack that ass." He tried to sound tough, but they both knew better.

"Ah, I see you haven't totally lost your manhood." She bit his lower lip and grabbed his swollen crotch. "Come on then tough guy, let's go," she said, licking her lips, pulled away from him. She pouted her full lips and slow walked backwards, down toward the old wooden stage. She smacked her ass that was wrapped in tight, worn jeans.

Tony watched her fade into the shadows but the little yellow light from his cheap ass Dollar Store flashlight traced her smoking hot frame down to the front of the stage.

"You are one cruel bitch, ya know that?" He forced a chuckle, adjusted his hard on and slowly followed.

"Hey babe, don't leave me alone in here, especially after what you did to me?" He grabbed her from behind, jamming his hard dick against her taught ass. He pressed her hard against the cold stage. She moaned, and then giggled.

Tony thought he heard a soft voice whisper from somewhere way off, backstage. He let the thought wash away into the blackness as she reached back and unzipped his jeans.

"Now that's what I was hoping to be doing tonight. Not fuckin' around some damn haunted movie shithole." He nibbled on her ear lobe and thrusted.

"Hey Babe, aren't you afraid that Howdy Doody will *jump* out and cut your balls off?" Alexis laughed and pulled away, leaving Tony's erect penis bouncing in the chilly darkness. She gave his testicles a playful squeeze and climbed up onto the stage, giggling.

"Now, that shit ain't right." Tony forced a laugh and covered his dick with his quivering hand and fought to see where his cock-tease of a girlfriend disappeared to.

"Follow me babe and I will make you see God," Tony heard Sherri's sensuous voice plead through the ebony, thick air. He still smelled something bad—something that reminded him of road kill out on Route 104—road kill as if they were a herd of mastodons. But there was another smell; a more powerful scent, that made him push all the Howdy Doody small town urban legend bullshit off into that shadows. The throbbing in his groin quickly helped him brush it aside. He needed to get laid.

Tony staggered as Sherri's flashlight disappeared into the darkness. He heard her lilting laughter further on in the blackness and the padding of hard soles from her Uggs boots on the wooden stage straight ahead of him.

"Hey babe, I always knew you wanted to be in the movies." His own voice causing him to jump as it filled up the thick silence. He waited a few long moments for a response. The silence was heavy and seemed to have a sound all its own; a low menacing hum filled his ears and sent a sharp jolt down his spine. He shivered and took a deep breath.

"Come on T-Rock, I'm sure we can find a couch or something back here and put that tiny thing of yours to use," Alexis' voice clawed through the darkness. "I know little-Tony isn't afraid of dark places."

Tony hopped up onto the stage and stopped as her sexy words we choked off behind the heavy curtains and torn screen.

Ssshh, Mr. Howdy, I think it's her—Alexis-Baby! Hold on, let me put the pack down and I'll go check. You stay here. Oh, you really want to come along? Ah. Mr. Howdy, uh...I don't think you should.

Okay, okay, but you have to promise, no, swear... Oh, better yet, pinky swear *not* to tell Mama anything, okay?

Cool beans. But you have to promise you won't make me hurt her like I did the others.

Pinky swear? Okay, it's a deal then.

I think I heard her over by the clothes room.

Let's go.

"Alexis, where are you, I have a little something for ya." Tony's voice died a mere few feet into the black foam of shadows that lay in front of him. He could hear Sherri's sultry giggles further in, once he passed the thick curtain of the stage. The air was thick and the same dead smell grew heavier, almost solid matter, caused him to gag and cover his mouth and nose with his sweaty hand.

"I'm so wet for you baby. If you don't hurry up, I'm gonna let big old Howdy Doody...do me!" Alexis moaned from further ahead.

"I'm comin' yo, and soon you will be too. You can bet your sweet ass on that one." Tony spat a gob of thick phlegm onto the crusted stage and shined the flashlight in the direction of his Alexis' sexy voice. It did little good. But once again, little tony did all the thinking as he pressed on into the ebon fabric of the backstage area.

<hr>

"Oh fuck me runnin'," Alexis bitched as the lemon-yellow beam from her flashlight flickered and snuffed out. She stopped quick and reached out to her right and her thin hands found purchase on the coolness of old brick. She leaned against the wall and slammed the flashlight against the wall and it retaliated by splitting open and spilling its guts of D batteries all over the hardwood floor. The metallic thud interrupted the thick silence. The echo was snatched up by the darkness and ushered away further into the backstage of the old theater.

"Tony, where the fuck are you, dumb ass?" She shouted and it bounced back to her with a harsh slap. The air was as thick as cement and just as heavy. The smell that welcomed them when they broke in was far worse back stage. Her arousal was long gone and now she shivered against the cold wall. It felt sticky to the touch and she recoiled and kicked at the rebellious batteries at her feet and cursed them.

"Tony!" She screamed out and it fell on a wall of black. She heard someone breathing.

She froze.

<hr>

My *willy* is growing again, Mr. Howdy. Alexis-Baby is close. I can smell her. Oh, that other smelly stuff? It's just...just my puppets. Ya know, the other folks who came to watch movies and cartoons. The ones who didn't want to go home. They don't talk much. They stink a little bit, but as you always tell me, they are enjoying the show.

I like making people happy. My smile grows so wide and feels like it will split my face in two, like the orange halves Mama used to pack for me in my Incredible Hulk lunch box. Well, that was before Mama pulled my out of school.

I like making people happy.
I can smell her.
My willy is wigglin', again.
Do I look handsome Mr. Howdy?
Alexis-Baby is gonna love me. I'm gonna make her happy.
Shhsshhhh! I can see her flashlight.
She's coming for me.
She will like it here with the others.
Alexis-Baby loves me.
Shhsshhhh.

"Hey babe, where the hell are you?" Tony waved his tiny flashlight like a Lightsaber in all directions but the darkness of backstage was as thick and unrelenting. A vigorous cold chill wracked his thin body; his erection long gone, turned into a turtle and found safety inside his body, next to his shrunken testicles. He gulped and looked about frantically in every direction for Alexis. She didn't answer and the beams from her flashlight were now gone. He didn't like this one damn bit.

"Quit fucking around. You know this shit ain't funny no more." He slowly walked forward. He had no clue where he was going. He was just following the path Alexis had been on before the black theater swallowed her. He hoped it was the right direction. His churning gut told him to run and get the hell away from this evil place. Alexis made mad jokes about it and the Howdy Doody killer and shit, but he believed it. He knew it to be true. He always had a sense for this kind of evil shit. And he knew he needed to find Alexis and his friends and get the hell out of there now.

A loud thudding came from ahead and off the left-somewhere behind the screen. He thought he heard her voice. He let loose a small smile at the comfort and headed that way off into even deeper darkness. Within it, his little light was lost.

Okay, you stay right here Mr. Howdy, she's comin' this way. Just wait to you see the look on her beautiful face.

I will make her happy.

"Sonofabitch," Alexis said, trying to peer into the darkness. It felt as if it was glaring back at her. *Just your imagine bitch. Get your shit together*, she told herself, her words feeling flat in the stifling air around her.

Tony was right. There was a really nasty stench in here. But it was worse backstage. The wave of what smelled like rotting meat and feces filled her nose and mouth. She fell to her knees and cupped her mouth. It was too late—the chewed remnants of a Big Mac and french fries flew out of her mouth and disappeared into the blackness. Her body convulsed and heaved.

She wiped her mouth and got her feet. Her knees buckled but she managed to keep her balance. Her stomach still felt like it had a million tiny MMA fighters in it, kicking the crap out of her. *If I could just see damnit.* She stood in complete darkness, wondering what to do next. A thought hit her like a lightning flash. She slapped herself in the side of the head and felt for her pants pocket.

"You can really be a dumb ass sometime ya know that Alexis Lynn Conroy!"

She pulled out her cell phone and flipped it open. Its bluish glow lit up her face and she found comfort in the cold color.

It didn't safe her from the stench that was redolent here, backstage. It reminded her of the north field of her uncle's cow farm where he dumped all the cattle that died or they had to kill if they were too sick to butcher. The stench of the rotting cows kept her from that part of the farm. But this smell was different. Too strong, too—

She held the cell phone in front of her. The soft light allowed her to make out only a few things a few feet in front of her; a few boxes, old mannequins, trash and empty beer cans. She slowly stepped forward and stopped sharply. A door painted in a sickly pale green. Like that of the color of green olive left out of the jar too long.

She tried the handle and it gave resistance, but relented and turned with a loud screech. She hoped that Tony might have heard it and would come to her. She thought about heading back the way she came, but was so turned around, she didn't know which way that was. The door was heavy and something seemed to be stopping her from opening it further. She put her shoulder into it and if belched a loud screech, and opened up.

The blue glow of her cell phone pierced the blackness of the room and it slipped from her trembling hand as the smell, unbearable outside the room was multiplied by a thousand as she once again, fell to her knees in spasms of revulsion and uncontrollable vomiting.

"Jesus Christ," Tony stood frozen in the same spot. A cloak of blackness surrounded him. He kept hearing a low, muttering voice but not sure where it was coming from. The damn theater was huge and filled with all kinds of shit and made sound travel strange. He didn't even know if he could trust his own ears. He thought Alexis was ahead but her flashlight was gone. Knowing her, she probably dropped the damned flashlight and that was the sound he had heard a few moments ago.

"Stupid girl is going to be the death of me." The words hung on his lips and he couldn't believe he said them. He let them go with a sharp shiver and decided to just keep walking straight ahead and he was certain he'd find her. Or at least hit a wall or something.

"Hey, what's the worst thing you could find here in this old, dark, condemned, rumored haunted fucking movie theater?" He shivered again—this one was more like a tremor than a cold chill. He swallowed hard and put one foot in front of the other and watched the piss-poor light bounce back at him as if it was an affront to its existence.

Tony cursed it and stepped cautiously into the gripping darkness.

"What the..." Alexis fought back the bile rising in her raw throat. She held the cell phone out in front of her and made a slow arc-staring in soul-shaking disbelief at the nightmarish scene inside the large room.

The ghoulish blue glow illuminated dozen of dead bodies; all strewn up in various, puppet-like poses all over the rot-filled wardrobe room—their blank stares and maggot-filled corpses welcomed her into their final home inside the Clark Theater. Her stomach twisted and acidic saliva filled her mouth as the light from her phone caught a family of engorged rats feasted on the stomach of a small boy, about the age of six, hanging only three feet from the entrance to this twisted Vaudevillian room from hell. His torn Pokémon shirt was stained deep red and ripped open to make easy dinning for the vermin crawling nonchalantly through what was left of his tiny intestines. More french fries flew from her mouth, peppering the dead boy and the oblivious rats feeding inside him.

She began to cry. Her head swam as fragments of horrific input flooded her mind. This must be fake; she tried to force herself to believe. She knew she was wrong. But the worst thought punched her in the gut. She spat puke and looked closer at the boy.

She knew him.

It was little Paulie Reynolds. She had babysat him. The local newspaper had reported that his drunk, psychotic father had kidnapped him and ran away to Canada. Her head swam with insane understanding as vomit filled her mouth again and she painted the blood and necrotic tissue covered floor with the finally remnants of her stomach.

"Oh poor Pau—oh my Go..." She heard something from the other side of the expansive room and froze. Her throat burned and she felt like fainting. She aimed the cell phone in the direction of the sound. She found nothing but more horror and stares from the dead.

She slowly moved the cell phone across the mass of the decomposing bodies and heard laughter. She stopped and felt her heart pounding. The air felt like concrete, squeezing her from all sides and she swung the phone back to the left, in the direction of the chilling sound.

"I make you happy Alexis-Baby,"

Was the last thing she heard.

Tony heard something coming from ahead—thought it was a scream or a cry, but wasn't sure. He quickened his steps but not by much. He didn't want to walk into a wall and knock his dumb ass out. The flashlight did its best but the steel-like darkness was much stronger than its little C-sized batteries could muster. The smell got worse as he moved deeper into the backstage area. His foot kicked something. He stopped, knelt down, and his hand found something cold.

"You have to be fuckin' kidding me?" He bitched as he fumbled the battery in his hand. He shook his head and chucked it behind him. It hit concrete and ricocheted back into the seats.

"Bitch is going to kill me, I swear to God." He continued on toward the source of the noise, straight ahead.

He had only moved a few feet when the faint, yellow beam from his flashlight exposed a faded green door, slightly open. He stopped. He heard something inside—a voice. A deep, childlike voice.

He leaned close. The door felt cold to the touch.

"*I know Mr. Howdy, put the needle through her hands first and THEN her feet. Jeepers' creepers, we have done this hundreds of times! You're starting to sound like Mama,*" The voice sounding like it came from the very blackest depths of Hell.

Tony fought to breathe.

"I told you. Alexis-Baby loves me. You see how she smiles and kisses me, Mr. Howdy?" The Satanic-child voice caused Tony's heart to squeeze and head flurry.

Ale—? He, it...has Alexis! The frantic thought overwhelming him.

He knew he had to do something. His pistol was in the glove compartment of his car; but there was no time for that shit.

He felt fucking stupid. He dug into his back pocket; ah fuck me, he reached for the other back pocked and found his cell phone and yanked it out and open it.

He punching in 9-1-1 and hit enter as he slowly shoved the slime green door all the way open.

"Motherfuck..." Tony couldn't speak, he couldn't move as he stared at the largest man— *thing*—he'd ever seen in his young life. It was a mountain-sized man that wore nothing but a knapsack and an orange, burlap sack hood, but it was what the creature had in his hands that caused his blood to freeze and breathe to fail him.

"Alexi—" was all he could mutter as he saw her naked body suspended in the middle of the room. Behind her, lay dozens of dead puppets, was the best image his fried brain could conjure up.

She was dead. Her chest was gapping open and her heart was missing. Blood was everywhere. It looked like a million gallon balloon filled with red paint exploded, slathering the room in her life blood.

The giant of a man turned its enormous head toward him. In his hands was a still-beating heart. Torrents of thick blood rained down from its cinder block-sized hands and mixed with the mangled flesh and bright white bones on the well-worn floor.

Alexis' heart—the one that only a few moments ago—loved him now was a midnight snack for the man-beast in front of him.

Tony snapped. He knew he should run in and kick the man-monster's ass, but he knew by the warm wetness spreading in his jeans, that his manhood left him a long time ago. Instead, he turned and ran the way he came, screaming and crying like the bitch he always knew he was and the only comfort he found was that of the voice from the 911 operator's voice on his cell telling him to stay on the line and that the police were on the way to his location.

He didn't stop running or pissing himself until he was safely outside the Clark Theatre and inside his car.

Where he wept uncontrollably and his sanity drifted away from him.

I got Alexis-Baby strung up real good just like you taught me Mr. Howdy. She looks pretty hanging up there, doesn't she? I think she looks happy. Just like all the others. But she ain't like them. No sir. She loves me 'cuz I make her happy.

I don't know where her jerk-face boyfriend went. I guess we scared him away. Too bad, 'cuz let me tell you, Mr. Howdy, that if I got my hands on him, he wouldn't be part of our Old Time, World Renowned Puppet Show, no sir! I would squash him and make his jerky body into mush! I don't like getting mad, Mr. Howdy, but I can't stand it when a boy hurts a girl! No way, no how! I'm okay, Mr. Howdy. I'll take a breath.

Mama?

Where is she?

Don't worry, Mr. Howdy. Mama is still away. We have time to play some more. We should find her boyfriend before he tells somebody, right Mr. Howdy?

Mr. Howdy? Where did you go?

You don't have to go! It's okay...wait...

What's that sound? Oh no...it's a police siren! More than one.

MAMA!!!

Mama...you there? I love you Mama! I need you.

Mr. Howdy just up and left me. Don't know where he went. He made me cry Mama!

He made me do bad things. Made Alexis-Baby and her stupid friends and all the others sleep black and string them up like little puppets. That ain't wrong, right Mama?

I never wanted to hurt no one... I just wanted to be me...to be left alone. Why do they hate me so much? I ain't no murderer! Dang it! I don't even know what that is.

I never meant to hurt nobody. All I want is to be left alone.

They have big guns and shiny badges. Telling me to get down and drop the knife. What did I do wrong, Mama?

They are hurting me and asking me questions. My head hurts, Mama. Please help me!

Why do they keep yelling and calling me names?

They're calling me a sick motherfucker, Mama. What does that mean?

I never wanted to hurt no one...I just wanted to be...to be left alone. Why do they hate me so much?

I ain't no murderer! Dang it. I don't even know what that is.

I never meant to hurt nobody and all I want is to be left alone.

What do I do, Mama? Please help me! Please tell me what to say.

I'm scared Mama!

You always know what to say, right Mama?
They call me a murderer Mama...a monster.
I ain't none of those things, wanna know why Mr. Police man?
"Mama says I'm no monster...
No Sir...She says I'm just an excitable boy!"

A year later, the headlines in the Sterling Point Chronicle read just that.
The 'Excitable Boy' serial killer was pronounced dead at 12:01am on Monday by lethal injection. He had no surviving family members.

ABOUT THE AUTHOR

Thomas A. Erb is a writer of dark fiction and suspense. He has other short stories and novellas being published in the near future and is hard at work on his next novel about foul monsters in the dead of winter. He also paints and illustrates murals of dark and fantastic imaginings. He lives in upstate New York with his wife Michelle and two dogs, Rask and Duchess. Find out more about the author at http://thomasaerb.webs.com/ and his blog http://taerb.blogspot.com/

ON FINE
FEATHERED WINGS

Gord Rollo

THE SUN WAS ALREADY SITTING LOW ON THE WESTERN HORIZON AS THE BIRDMAN began his difficult climb up the sixteen foot high chain link prison fence, freedom on his feverish mind and a mess of sticky black feathers glued to his skeletal-thin body.

No; not *that* Birdman.

No; not *that* prison.

Robert Stroud had long since left his iron-barred perch in San Francisco Bay for that great big birds nest in the sky, but unlike the famous Birdman of Alcatraz, Nickolas Denko planned to make it out of his cage without having to sit around waiting until he died. In fact, he wasn't sitting around waiting for anything.

He was going to fly.

Up and up Nicholas climbed, his grip on the fence precarious at best, all the interlaced feathers stuck on his hands and feet not making this as easy as he'd hoped. In his head, he'd pictured scaling the high fence in seconds, unfurling his majestic homemade wings and posing just for a moment in the last dying rays of twilight for guards and fellow inmates alike to gape at with wonder and awe at his avian body. And then before anyone could react, launching into the open night sky; the icy November wind blowing in from the north catching his fall and lifting him high above the astonished crowd gathered below. He'd maybe give them all one last wave as he flapped his dark wings once, twice, three powerful times and banked left out over the prison wall heading for the new life that awaited him on the other side. Freedom; in every possible way imaginable, was his for the taking and no one could...

...Nicolas' left hand slipped, several long black feathers drifting to the hard concrete surface of the yard below, the rest of him barely managing to cling to the steel mesh and avoid the plunge himself.

Stay focused, he reminded himself. *Your plans don't mean shit if you smash your skull open before you even start.*

The Birdman took a deep breath to slow down his racing heart and began to climb again, more determined than ever to leave this hell hole behind forever. Stillwater Prison could kiss his feathered ass goodbye, as far as he was concerned.

Hand over hand.

The fence freezing cold between his toes and on the bottoms of his bare feet.

On the outskirts of Oak Park Heights, Minnesota, the state's worst offenders are housed in a 443 inmate, nine unit maximum security penitentiary more commonly known as Stillwater Penitentiary, acknowledged by many in the system to be America's hardest prison. Inside this Level 5 (maximum) facility Nicholas has been declared by a board of physicians to be a delusional schizophrenic with obsessive compulsive tendencies and resides with 52 other unbalanced men in the Mental Health Unit. The MHU is still maximum security and nearly as nasty as the other lockdown units here but the inmates inside the MHU aren't segregated and have access to the facility's exercise yard for two hours every morning and night.

Staring out that chain link fence at the fields beyond every day for the past six years has twisted thirty-eight year old Denko's mind even further from center than it had been when he arrived here, a common run of the mill sex offender from nearby St. Paul. On the outside, it had been the pre-teen girls he'd obsessed over, but with children removed from his world now, it's the birds that have earned his warped sense of love. The crows, to be specific.

The inmates in here are terrible to him; mercilessly taunting, beating, and raping him whenever the guard's backs are turned. Not that the screws are any better; the guards as mean as the convicts, the only way to tell them apart are the uniforms. The crows take Nicholas away from all that pain and humiliation. Watching the glorious dark birds circle in the sky above Stillwater has given him many wonderful thoughts spinning around in his troubled mind, grand dreams of a fantasy life far away from this frigid place.

And then one day back in March of last year, Nicholas started to notice the long black feathers that fell from the sky and blew around on the ground; precious gifts from his feathered friends and previously tossed as trash by the clean-up crews who raked the grass and swept the concrete yard on a daily basis. It was only a matter of time before Nicholas volunteered for the job and the first scratches of a desperate plan began to form in his disturbed mind. The birds didn't shed feathers all year long, of course, but it seemed they'd drop one here and there regardless of the season, perhaps just for him. In his dementia, it meant the crows were supporting him; speeding his plan along, helping any way they could. They had a connection you see; Nicholas and the crows. He didn't understand it yet, but even back then he knew that it was true.

Knew that it was special.

Nicholas immediate went on a severe diet and exercise plan, literally starving himself to lose as much weight as possible and transforming his already thin body into a shell of skin and bones. Lean and mean was the plan. The lighter the better, regardless of what the doctors told him. He also began storing as many feathers as he could collect, eventually filling a small storage area beneath the stairs in the janitorial department where he kept his rake and brooms. As crazy as his idea for escape might seem to some, the Birdman was bound and determined to succeed.

The Birdman finally clawed his way to the top of the fence, freedom only a few flaps of his wings away. He stood to his full 6' 2" height upon the top rail, using only the metal light post beside his left hand to help him balance. The fence's steel barbs cut into the tender bottoms of his feet and the chilly wind blew right through his carefully applied layers of feathers and stung his naked flesh beneath but none of that mattered anymore. Those sensations were just pain and Nicholas had been dealing with that all his life. All the Birdman cared about was that first exhilarating moment of flight, the moment he'd been waiting on for the past twenty months.

"Caw...CAW!" he shouted into the sky, letting his friends in the fields beyond know he was on his way. In his heart, he truly believed the crows understood his squawks and would be expecting him soon. Some of the big black birds were already circling high above the prison, urging him on.

Carefully turning around, he spread his dark wings for the people below, reenacting the scene he'd dreamt about for so long, only now that his moment of glory was finally here the guards and prisoners gathered below weren't looking at him in wonder and awe as he'd expected.

They were all laughing.

Pointing their fingers and laughing like they'd never seen anything so funny in all their lives. Nicholas could maybe understand that from the inmates; they were certifiably crazy after all, but why were the prison guards making fun of him? Shouldn't they, at the very least, be trying to stop him from escaping?

Unless they're jealous. Yeah, that was it. Jealous of his beautiful wings and the fact he'd been smart enough to best them. *Screw them all. I'm outta here...*

The Birdman bent his feathered knees and prepared to launch.

The truth of the matter was that everyone had known about Nicholas' plan pretty much from the start. The prisoners didn't give a rat's ass what the skinny little bastard did with his fucked up life, so they just used and abused him the same as they'd done for his first four years at Stillwater. The guards probably should have cared, should have put a stop to this long before now when they found his stash of crow feathers and glue but they were a hardened, cruel bunch of men who hoped for something interesting to break the monotony on most days. To a man, they'd been waiting for this day to happen, hoping Denko was stupid enough to try. They'd all watched the skinny nutcase admiring those damn birds on the other side of the fence, making these stupid 'caw' noises as if he was actually talking to the brainless beasts. The guards could have taken his feathers any time they'd wanted. They could have removed him from the yard clean-up crew too.

Hell they could even have shot him dead as soon as he started climbing the chain link fence tonight but it wasn't everyday they'd get a chance to see a grown man butt-naked and covered in crow feathers take a header off the top of the fence. Right or wrong, they were just as curious as the rest of the inmates to see if Denko would actually have the balls to go through with it.

"Jump...jump...jump," the sadistic crowd began to chant.

Nicholas hated them for it; a white hot rage building within him, knowing full well what they were hoping was going to happen. Too bad he was planning on disappointing them. A satisfied smirk touched the edges of his mouth.

The Birdman leaped out into open air, screeching at the top of his lungs as the joy of freedom coursed through his veins, the adrenaline rush as strong as the cold north wind blowing in his face. The wind caught under his homemade wings and for a moment he knew he'd been right all along, knew he'd proven to everyone in this damn place that he wasn't crazy and that no one deserved to be caged up like this. He started to flap his mighty wings and...

...and Nicholas plummeted toward the unforgiving concrete below.

Sixteen feet isn't a huge height to fall from; certainly survivable, but the Birdman hit hard; still pitifully looking skyward and trying to piston his feathered arms up and down in what he thought was a crow-like manner. The left side of his body absorbed most of the impact, therefore taking the most damage, shattering the stick-thin lower bones in his leg just above his ankle. The noise of his Tibia and Fibula bones shattering together could be heard all over the prison yard, sounding like a pair of china tea cups being simultaneously smashed beneath a cinder block. The rest of Nicholas' thin body thumped down on top of his damaged leg causing the broken bones to agonizingly scrape together like fingernails on a chalkboard, the noise loud enough that some of the closest onlookers could hear it over the din of the crowd. Nicholas screamed so loud and intensely that the remainder of the murder of crows in the field beyond were startled enough to take to the air squawking, but eventually his injured left leg went numb and his agonizing screams slowly tapered off to quiet whimpers.

And that was when the noise of the crowd broke through the pain and suffering he was enduring and Nickolas heard everyone laughing again. No one moved to help him, but many inmates rushed up and ripped a handful of crow feathers off his back or off his legs and chest; anywhere they could grab a souvenir of this night's festivities for when the inevitable rumors started spreading. By noon tomorrow, the entire penitentiary would have heard about the Birdman's spectacular non-flight and they wanted a piece of the infamous moment to prove they'd actually been there.

Hank Brubaker, the head screw on the yard tonight, eventually tossed everyone off inmate Denko, and stood over top of the half-naked man weeping on the ground. If Nicholas thought he was about to receive some much needed care he was mistaken. The burly guard called him a "Stupid crazy fuck!" and kicked him in the ribs with his heavy black boots. Something broke inside Nickolas' left side; two maybe three ribs popping like gunshots in the cold night air, and he turned on his good side to vomit a mouthful of thick syrupy bile.

"Get up!" Brubaker said, the guard showing no sympathy for what he'd just done. "You want medical aid...you can drag your own raggedy feathered ass to the doctor's."

Nicholas thought there was no way he could possibly get to his feet on his own but he knew he'd better try or the brutal head screw would make an example of him again if he had to. Brubaker had probably enjoyed the ridiculous escape attempt but the show was over and Nicholas could tell by the familiar look in the guard's eyes that he was done fooling around. All Nicholas wanted to do was close his eyes and go to sleep, but just as he was preparing himself to take another beating, he glanced skyward and notices that above them hundreds of crows were circling the yard, cheering him on with their strange high-pitched voices, giving him strength he never knew he had.

Screw you, Brubaker, Nicholas thought. *Screw all of you.*

With an effort bordering on Herculean, the Birdman somehow found a way to stand up, supporting his weight on his right leg and leaving his ruined left to dangle at an odd angle, the skin swollen purple above his ankle, visible through the patchy group of feathers that remained. Brubaker and everyone else present were clearly surprised when he made it to his feet, but surprise turned to shock when instead of hobbling toward the infirmary, Nicholas started hopping back toward the chain link fence. As incredible as it seemed, he started climbing for the sky again, gritting his teeth in agony as he pulled himself higher and higher on one leg and a chest that felt like it was being stabbed with an ice pick every time he tried to inhale.

When he paused to rest, he glanced over his shoulder and saw Brubaker shaking his head in disgust, waving his men off, but not doing anything to stop him. The inmates were cheering him on, thrilled that they might actually get a chance to see a repeat performance. Nicholas whispered a quick prayer to the birds circling above and started climbing again, ignoring the pain in his side and concentrating on nothing but putting one hand above the other.

In time, Nicholas made it all the way back to the top of the fence, again using the light post to help him balance on the rail. He spread his beautiful homemade wings again, always the showman, and noticed the rips and tears and gaping holes torn in them from the inmates' earlier thievery. *Bastards!* If it was the last thing he ever did, he'd like to make them all pay for their ignorance, cruelty, and laughter.

A wave of dizziness hit Nicholas and he nearly lost his grip on the light post. When he regained his balance, he looked down to see Brubaker smiling at him, clearing enjoying his misery.

"Well go ahead and get it over with," the head screw shouted. "We haven't got all night. Do us all a favor and try land on your head this time!"

Everyone started laughing and began their "Jump...jump," chant again. Every eye on the yard was looking Nicholas' way, but he was ignoring them. His eyes were looking straight up, focusing on the thick mass of dark birds swirling around and around above him. Maybe he was hallucinating but it looked like barely visible lightning bolts were flashing from one bird to another, tiny tendrils of wispy power bouncing at random amongst the crows and drifting down toward his outstretched wings. Was he only kidding himself that he could feel and even smell an unnatural electricity in the air around him; that special connection between him and the crows perhaps. His homemade feathers ruffling in the breeze as if they were really a part of his body, rising in excitement like the hair on the back of his neck.

"Help me," the Birdman whispered, his broken ribs making it nearly impossible to draw a deep enough breath to shout. "Help me!"

And the crows did.

The birds dropped out of the sky in groups of twenty or thirty, sweeping in wave after wave to form a living black-winged blanket around Nicholas' shape, digging into the soft flesh of his arms, legs, chest, and back with their long-taloned feet, but leaving his head and eyes exposed. The pain was mind-numbing but he accepted their hooks happily, instinctively knowing this was the way things were supposed to be. It took less than a minute for hundreds of crows to cover Nicholas from throat to toes, joining their primitive minds and flesh with his, finally forming the real Birdman of Stillwater Penitentiary. The agony of his injures and the birds' claws began to fade away, a warm sensation of strength flooding into his core, like someone had reached within his soul and turned on a secret power switch. On a thousand fine feathered wings, Nicholas easily took to the air, rejoicing in his ability to defy gravity like in his most cherished dreams but having no intention of flying away from the prison yet.

The prey had become the predator now and he had other things in mind.

The Birdman descended on the inmates and guards like a prehistoric beast, all beaks and sharp claws, biting and tearing anyone in sight. Flesh peeled from the inmates' faces and blood poured from the guards' open throats, the Birdman's wrath choosing no favorites on this cold November night. One by one, bodies dropped to the concrete yard, the screams of the dying echoing across the open fields to the south.

Without an ounce of pity or remorse, the Birdman took his vengeance, painting the prison yard red with the blood of those who had tormented and beat him for years. He saved Brubaker for last; using his powerful new living legs to grab the guard around his waist and lift him high into the air. He flew up twenty feet, forty, and then hovered in place a full eighty feet above the ground. Blood streamed down Brubaker's chest and legs as he tried to break free but when he realized how high he was dangling above the prison yard he stopped fighting in a hurry. Dozens of razor sharp black beaks continued to peck away at his skin where ever they came in contact with his body.

"Don't do it," Brubaker cried out in panic. "Please...you can't!"

The Birdman began to laugh.

"Fly, you bastard...be free!"

The Birdman released his hold on the guard and Brubaker immediately dropped like a rock, his muscular body picking up tremendous speed as he rocketed toward the concrete below. The part of Nicholas' conscience that was still his own didn't really want to watch the impact, but the bird-of-prey part of his brain refused to let him turn his eyes away. Brubaker hit the concrete like a two hundred pound bag of rotted vegetables, his skull shattering into gooey grey-red fragments and his belly opening up like a hand grenade had gone off inside his stomach, splattering the bloody soup that had previously been his innards in a circular pattern nearly fifteen feet in every direction.

His bloodlust finally sated, the Birdman banked left and rode a current of frigid air heading south, smiling as he crossed over the boundaries of the prison and flew out over open fields. Now that the slaughter was over and the adrenaline rush starting to fade, some of the pain from his damaged body was registering in his brain again. His mind and body link with the crows began to break down and the birds started releasing their hold on him, flying away on their own. His body weight, light as he was, soon was too much for the remaining birds and they began to lose altitude. Not a freefall, but the more black birds that let go, the faster he began to drop. Luckily, he made it back to solid ground, thankful not all his friends had abandoned him at the same time. Soon the remaining crows released their hold on him and without their support he collapsed onto the dirt of the field, his body a ruin of broken bones and a thousand bloody puncture wounds where the birds' claws had joined with his flesh.

Nicholas tried to get to his feet once, but his left leg and side were on fire and he was light-headed from the loss of blood. His frail body shook from the cold as he tried reaching out to his feathered friends again, using his voice as well as his mind, trying to make that same blessed connection they'd just had but it wasn't to be. None of the crows came to his aid and he realized that this very likely was the end of the line. If he didn't die from his numerous injuries and wounds, he'd surely freeze to death out here before the guards found him. There was no plan 'B' and no way of going back to the pitiful life he'd known before; not that he wanted that even if he could have it. Strangely, he was okay with his situation, finally at peace and ready to leave this rotten world.

But then one of the crows swooped down and sat on his bleeding chest.

And then another one.

Ten more following closely behind.

Soon all of Nicholas' friends were back, a smarm of dark crows sitting on top and beside his shaking body, snuggling close to each other and pressing their feathered bodies up against his exposed skin. They even sat upon his face and throat, leaving nothing visible of his broken body except for his mouth and nose. Amazing as it seemed, they were trying to comfort him, forming a living blanket of feathers to keep him warm. It worked too; Nicholas began to sense that unnatural electricity again and instantly felt much better. His dizziness faded away and his broken bones went numb again, exactly like when he'd been flying; their unexplainable connection giving Nicholas the power to either block out the injuries, or dare he think it—the capability to start healing them.

Darkness spread across the land and with Nicholas completely covered head to toe in jet black birds he was virtually invisible. Despite the frigid wind blowing across the field and the rock hard dirt below his back, the Birdman had never felt more comfortable and loved in his entire life. He was fast asleep in seconds.

After a futile search of the surrounding woods for the better part of the night, the understandably shaken day shift guards eventually noticed an unusual mound of crows sitting silently on top of one another about half way into an open dirt field just south of the prison. It was such a peculiar sight; and after being called in early to be briefed on the incomprehensible and bloody events of last night, several of the guards decided to go investigate the scene. From the prison wall at least, it appeared as if the crows were purposely concealing something beneath their dense numbers. Or some*one*. It was a crazy notion, but so was everything else about inmate Denko's impossible escape.

Four heavily armed guards walked out into the field but try as they might, they couldn't get the crows to fly away and let them see what lay on the ground beneath. It took two loud blasts from a shotgun to finally startle the birds into flight, scattering the murder in all directions, squawking their displeasure as they left the field in angry groups. When the last big black bird took to the air, the guards were left looking down at...

...nothing.

The Birdman was gone.

Four well-trained, experienced guards stood in the field nervously looking at each other, all of them knowing Nicholas Denko was still at large and considered extremely dangerous. The escaped madman could be anywhere by now but it was a telling sign that not one of them looked across the field to the dense thicket of woods beyond; the most likely place a desperate criminal might try and hide. No; to a man all four of the Stillwater guards tilted their heads to search the sky above, secretly hoping there would be nothing up there to see.

ABOUT THE AUTHOR

Gord Rollo was born in St. Andrews, Scotland, but has lived in Southern Ontario, Canada since 1971. His short stories and novella-length work have appeared in many pro and semipro publications throughout the genre and he is currently nearing the end of a four book novel contract with Leisure Books in New York City. His novels include: *The Jigsaw Man, Crimson, Strange Magic,* and *Valley Of The Scarecrow.* Besides novels, Gord edited the acclaimed evolutionary horror anthology, *Unnatural Selection: A Collection of Darwinian Nightmares.* He also co-edited *Dreaming of Angels,* a horror/fantasy anthology created to increase awareness of Down's syndrome and raise money for research. He's hard at work on his next novel tentatively entitled *The Translators* and can be reached through his website at www.gordqrollo.com.

IN DARKER WATERS

Robert Ford

"The King is dead."

Emmett Stevens turned on the lamp and fumbled for his glasses on the nightstand. "Who the hell—?"

"It's Smitty. You better get down to the lake."

"It's four thirty in the goddamned morning."

"Sorry Emmett, but you're gonna want to take a look at this."

Emmett let out a sigh, looking forward to his impending retirement. Small town or not, sometimes being the sheriff was a pain in the ass. When Emmett had taken office, sheriff Walder had handed over his badge and pistol with a smile. "Every day is like walking blind in a pasture. You never know whether you're going to step in a pile of shit or not." It was the truest advice Emmett had ever received in his life.

Emmett wondered if he would follow Walder's lead after he retired; pack up the roost and head down to Florida. Probably not, he thought. Christmas lights wrapped around palm trees just seems…unchristian.

"All right, Smitty. I'll bring a thermos of coffee for us." Emmett hung up the phone while Smitty was still talking.

"Everything ok?" Ruthie turned over in bed, shielding her eyes against the glare of the lamp.

"Smitty's rambling on about The King being… never mind, baby. Go back to sleep. I'll be back soon as I can."

He leaned down and gave his wife of thirty-seven years a kiss on the lips. "I love you."

"Love you too, hon." Ruthie turned back over and pulled the blankets tighter.

Emmett let out another sigh as he pulled on his uniform and gear. They felt heavier every day.

Palm tree Christmas or not, Florida was looking better all the time.

❧ ☙

Mist was rising off the murky water of Lake Branson as Emmett pulled the cruiser to a stop next to the loading slip. Wes Southard's pickup was parked halfway down the concrete ramp, boat still on the trailer. In the distance, the sun started to brighten the horizon. The maples and oaks on the hillside were becoming silhouettes.

Smitty crouched next to something bulky and glistening on the water banks. Tom Holloway was there too, but of course that was a given. The way Holloway gossiped down at the barbershop, there wasn't a mouse fart in town he didn't know about.

Fishing rod in his hand, Wes Southard stood next to Tom. Both men looked lost and confused. Scared.

What the hell is going on?

Emmett grabbed the thermos of coffee and some foam cups from the stack on his passenger seat and got out.

"Morning Emmett."

"Boys." He nodded and started to offer cups but caught sight of whatever Smitty was kneeling beside.

My God. What in the blue hell...

The King had already been a legend when Emmett was a young boy. He had never seen him firsthand, but there were countless tales of how he had busted line after line, escaping even the most skilled fishermen.

The closest Emmett had come was a few years back when Raymond Gover had driven his sooped-up Nova into the lake after drinking until closing time at the Wishing Well.

They'd had to call in a diver from Franklin County. Five minutes in and the man had damned near broken his neck getting out of the lake, shaking like he'd seen Lucifer himself. Never knew if it was true or not, but the man smelled like he had let loose in his wet suit.

Fact was; the diver had come face to face with The King. The legends described the catfish as eight feet long with a mouth that could gulp down a basketball.

The legends were wrong. The King was bigger.

Emmett knelt down for a closer look and Smitty angled his flashlight so he could see better.

The King's eyes were milky white with death and as big as Blue Willow china saucers. Whiskers the thickness of corn stalks sprouted from the front of its snout.

A thick inner tube tongue the color of trading card bubble gum lined a mouth wide enough to swallow Emmett whole, and that was saying something. Lord knew, over the years, he'd had his share of second helpings at dinner and his waistline showed it.

But what held Emmett's attention—what made him understand the fear in the men's faces—was the rest of The King's slime-covered body. It was as big around as a grown dairy cow and would have easily extended a full twelve feet if it hadn't been torn completely in half.

The fish's spine had been shredded. Its skin glistened in ragged tatters around the stump of his body. One pectoral fin was completely ripped off, leaving behind a raw pink stub.

Smitty moved to aim the beam of the flashlight inside the carcass. Emmett could see the oily collection of The King's innards and was suddenly glad he hadn't had breakfast yet.

Emmett stood up and let out a low whistle.

"What the hell did this, Emmett?" Tom's voice was shaky. The man wasn't questioning for the inside scoop—he was scared.

Hell, Emmett had seen Tom and his kids jumping off the docks and swimming in these same waters barely a month ago.

Wes stared with wide glassy eyes at what was left of The King. Something in the man's expression proclaimed he was taking a break from fishing for quite a while.

Emmett took his hat off and stepped to the edge of the lake. A memory started to break the still surface of Emmett's mind and he forced it back down to the shadows where it belonged.

Smitty stepped up beside him, just out of range of the other men.

"Emmett?" he whispered.

Sunrise was about to break and soon the water would mirror the clear blue sky. For now, nothing but black ink stretched off into the depths of the lake, following the dogleg of hillside toward Bentley Springs.

Both Emmett and the lake had nothing to say.

Carl Mattigan shuffled down the hallway toward the kitchen, hoping Sarah had left him some coffee before she left for work. The house was quiet except for the sound of SpongeBob Squarepants in the living room. Robbie ate a bowl of cereal while his gaze stayed glued to the TV screen.

"Don't you ever get tired of SpongeBob?"

Robbie smiled and shook his head.

He's got my smile, Carl thought, returning Robbie's grin. *Eyes too. Boy's gonna get more ass than a barstool when he gets older.*

"Y'know, back in the day, Bugs Bunny would've kicked the crap out of SpongeBob." Carl feinted a punch to Robbie's stomach, making the boy giggle and reflexively protect himself.

"Riding your bike to school again?"

"Yep. After SpongeBob's over."

Carl winked at his son and walked into the kitchen. The coffee pot had a half-inch of weak looking coffee left in it. *Goddamn it, woman.*

Still groggy, Carl made a fresh pot, sat down at the kitchen table and shook a Winston from his pack. The newspaper was folded to the HELP WANTED section, Sarah's idea of giving him a nudge.

For Chrissakes, I only got pink-slipped two days ago!

Every year it was the same thing at Finnley Construction. As fall approached, work slowed down until the layoffs began. This year was no different, just a little lighter than usual. But with the damned economy in the shitter, he couldn't expect to be busy. He and Randy Fuhrman had been laid off yesterday at quitting time. It came as a surprise, but after twelve years working a backhoe at the same company, it damn sure shouldn't have.

Sarah was trying to get him to find another job over the winter months, but what the hell for?

Screw that shit. I'll sit on my ass and collect unemployment for a while. Bad enough for nine months out of the year my back feels like it's going to fall apart when I stand up from the shitter. Having a backhoe jack hammering my goddamn spine eight hours a day ain't easy work. Let the government pay for a little winter vacation R & R. Sounds like a mighty fine idea to me.

By the time spring comes around, work will start up again. Always has. Always will. Sarah can just shut the hell up about it if she knows what's good for her.

Carl checked the status of the coffee pot and looked at the stack of dirty dishes in the sink. He tossed the classifieds aside and glanced at the front-page headline. Unemployment Claims Rise For The Fifth Month In A Row.

"No shit, Sherlock. You can add me to the list next month."

"What, Daddy?" Robbie called from the other room.

"Daddy's just talkin' to himself, buddy. Done with your Lucky Charms?"

SpongeBob must have gotten interesting because Robbie ignored the question.

A grainy picture of Wes Southard standing in front of the lake was on the LOCAL STORIES page. Carl read the headline and studied the photo. Slowly, he folded the newspaper and set it down on the kitchen table.

He sat there for a long while, his eyes glazed over as he became lost in thought. His cigarette burned down to the filter as it rested in the ashtray, then went out on its own. The coffee pot finished brewing and went ignored. Robbie came in with his bowl of cereal and Carl never noticed him.

Twenty-five years and it's back again.

Carl smiled to himself, and reached for the phone.

"Randy?"

"What do you want, dickhead?"

"Fuck you. We're goin' catfishin' tonight. Get your shit and meet me at the lake around nine o'clock."

"I'm on call at the fire station tonight." Randy was crunching something, probably those damned barbecue pork rinds he always had a bag of.

"Have them put you on call. Ain't gonna be a damn thing happenin' until Halloween and you know it. Then you're gonna be so busy you won't even have time to whack off."

Carl lit a fresh cigarette.

"C'mon, Randy. I'll get the bait. You pick up a couple o' six packs. Be like old times before we had kids 'n shit."

"I ain't got no kids."

"Only 'cause your wife's got an ice box for a cooch."

"I'd tell you to kiss my ass, but you're right."

"C'mon man." Carl took a drag, blowing smoke out for a dramatic pause. "I'll even bring the last of my stash."

The phone was quiet. Even Randy's crunching paused.

"Lyin' son of a bitch! You told me you were dry last week!"

"I know, but I only got a little bit and with both of us gettin' laid off who the hell knows when we'll be able to catch a buzz next?"

"I'll be there."

The phone clicked dead and Carl hung up the receiver. He smiled and shut his eyes in silent thanks.

Emmett leaned back in his chair, put his feet on his desk and started sifting through the photographs for the fourth time. They still showed him the same damned thing he'd seen in person earlier this morning. He tossed them on his desk.

When they got back to the station, Smitty had been scraping up every last reason he could for what happened to The King.

Somebody's motorboat blade hit it.

A bear wandered out of territory and went after the catfish.

The King got caught in one of the water turbines at the dam and was cut in half.

Horseshit, Emmett thought. All of them, horseshit. He reached into his desk drawer and pulled a pint of Jack Daniels out, tilting it to the head for a healthy swallow before he stashed it away again.

A motorboat blade would have to be four feet long to be able to cut the body like that.

In all his life, Emmett had never heard of a bear coming down this far.

And the water turbines at the dam? No way. The King's body would likely be mashed to chum from all the pressure.

Emmett looked at his desk drawer, deciding if he needed another swallow of whiskey to deal with what kept coming back to his thoughts. He resisted the pull of the liquor and released a deep sigh, fighting the memory of what he'd seen twenty-five years ago.

Emmett felt himself shaking inside, fear snaking up his spine. When he admitted defeat, everything came flooding back.

A few months after Emmet became sheriff, his mother had lost an eight-month battle with cancer and being an only child, he had to take care of all the arrangements. It was a hell of a crutch to pick as a sheriff but he'd taken to carrying a flask in his jacket.

Ruthie had helped him as best she could, but Emmett was still in emotional turmoil. Relief because his mother was finally at rest, but guilty as hell because he felt relief. Anger because he had to do so many damned things before he could even let himself grieve. The night before her funeral, he had barely sat down with a bottle of Mr. Daniels when the call came in.

Kids had been swimming down at the lake. One of them, Tommy Mattigan, went under and didn't come back up.

Emmett remembered the call as clear as anything. The way Connie at dispatch had sounded. The fear in her voice. She had kids of her own and Emmett knew what was going through her mind. Connie quit not too long after that call. It took a certain kind of person to emotionally deal with all the reports to the station. He guessed after Tommy died, Connie realized she wasn't that kind of person after all.

Emmett couldn't blame her. One of the worst things about his job was telling a parent I'm sorry. No two words ever felt as inadequate in that situation as they did.

When Emmett got there, the two boys at the lake were scared shitless and in shock. The medics had bundled them in blankets and somebody had given them hot chocolate. The older Mattigan boy's eyes kept scanning the lake, searching for something.

They called in divers and searched the lake all the way down to the dam. Nothing. Not a goddamn thing.

Insult to injury? *Having an empty coffin at your kid's funeral.*

Emmett hadn't known the Mattigans, as they had only moved in earlier that year, but he went to pay his respects just the same. Hell, half the damn town had. It was one of the things he loved about living here. The people took care of their own.

Emmett sat in his cruiser for a while, taking swigs from his flask and working up the courage to walk inside. When the whiskey was gone, he went into the church, sat in the back row and listened to Pastor Phil talk about the Lord's newest angels living in the mansion of God. When Tommy Mattigan's mother broke into screams and crumpled into a ball in the church aisle, Emmett had had enough.

He slipped outside and went straight to a liquor store, upgraded to a fifth and drove to the lake, walked out on the dock and sat down.

Emmett took his hat off and felt the breeze against his damp head. He thought about the two deaths in the past week. His mother, older, but still gone way before her prime. The boy, barely nine years old, sucked down into the darkness before he had a real chance to see life.

His anger grew until Emmett screamed out over the water, wordless shrieks of fury at God, life, death and the unfairness of everything. The justice of nothing.

Tears streamed down his face. He gave one last bellow of rage and lifted the bottle of whiskey to throw it far out into the lake.

That's when Emmett saw it.

On the far bank, a young doe stood at the water's edge. She must have decided Emmett wasn't a danger with the stretch of lake separating them, and she bent down to get a drink.

And the lake came alive.

Filthy dregs of muck at the edge of the lake unfurled into a thick mass the size of a Winnebago camper and dropped as a cloak over the slender neck of the doe. It *opened her up* and blood began to gush in torrents from the stump of her neck.

A tangle of rust colored legs was the last Emmett saw of the deer as she thrashed wildly and the dark mass pulled her under the surface of the lake.

Emmett could make out limbs beneath the muddy slick, rippled and lean with muscle. He dropped the bottle of whiskey and it thunked against the wooden dock before rolling into the placid water with a heavy splash.

It turned slowly and looked at him. There were eyes beneath the twists of water reeds and sludge. Glowing pupils, reptilian and ancient, calculating eyes that were predatory and patient.

Emmett pissed himself right there on the dock.

The creature submerged and Emmett watched as air bubbles hit the surface and a frothy wake began rapidly heading toward him. Emmett broke into a run, his back cold with gooseflesh and fear that he had only felt before as a young child. He made it to his cruiser and fumbled with the keys before gunning the car out of there.

He didn't stop trembling until he made it home and crawled into bed with Ruthie. She held him warm and close and ran her hands tenderly over his head when he cried against like a child. Emmett let her think they were tears of grief. It was easier that way.

Over the years he'd done well at burying the memory of that day at the lake, talking himself into believing it wasn't real. It was the whiskey, the grief, the stress of everything. Tears brimmed along the edges of Emmett's eyes and spilled down over his cheeks.

He knew better.

Emmett reached into his desk and took out the bottle of Jack for one more swallow. He couldn't look at the photos anymore. He couldn't pull out the yellowed newspaper clippings hidden at the back of his desk drawer talking about the Mattigan boy's death.

Ruthie's warm embrace and tender hands would never ease the hard facts. The plain truth was the world was full of monsters. The things that go bump in the night are real.

He took off his badge and laid it on top of his desk beside his duty hat, then undid his utility belt and folded it across his desk calendar.

"Good-bye, Ruthie."

Moments later, Smitty walked in to see Emmett still crying as he shoved the barrel of his service revolver into his mouth. A moment after that, Sheriff Emmett finally found peace.

Crickets chirped like toy whistles around the lake. Carl cracked a cold Budweiser and handed it to Randy, then opened another for himself. The Coleman lantern cast a harsh yellow-green glow over his face. He pointed to a cove on the far side of the lake.

"Let's head over there. I'll pack us a bowl and we'll get things baited."

"Been a long time, buddy." Randy grinned and steered the boat where Carl had pointed.

"Hell yeah. When's the last time we went out like this? Shit...five years maybe?" Carl packed some weed from a plastic baggie into a small wooden pipe, lit up and took a hit.

Randy nodded and ran his hands over his scraggly excuse for a beard. He cut the motor and let the boat drift as he took the bowl from Carl and inhaled, releasing a plume of thick smoke.

Like most nights, the water was dead still. Carl looked around. They were roughly twenty feet from the bank and the glow of the lantern caught highlights of some of the trees. Maple leaves floated in the black water. Fire red and lemon yellow; a handful of party confetti drifting endlessly.

"Ever think about him?" Randy asked the question in a soft voice. He kept his gaze focused on his rod and bait.

Carl felt his heart thumping harder. He bit back a smile. He tapped the pipe over the edge of the boat and put it back in his jacket pocket. He took a slow, deep breath of fresh air in his lungs and exhaled the same way.

"Sometimes." He finished off his first beer and opened a fresh one. "Try not to. His birthday's hard though."

"I'm an asshole, man. I shouldn't have brought it up. Just being back here and all..." Randy cast his rod, staring out after it.

"Did you mean for that thing to get him, Randy? It got The King, y'know? I read about it in this morning's paper. Bit that ol' catfish clean in half."

"I don't know what you're talking about, man. Tommy drowned, that's it." Randy stared at the water. His fishing line shone like spider web.

"A stupid accident. That's all it was." Carl quietly turned his fishing rod around and gripped the shaft like a sword. "After you pushed him off the dock to save your own ass, did you see Tommy's face when that thing pulled him under?" Carl whispered the words. "I did."

Randy turned and Carl swung, catching him square on the cheekbone with his reel. The skin split to the bone, spurting blood down his face. Randy fell toward the side of the boat and Carl swung back again, catching him against the temple.

Randy outweighed him by a good thirty pounds, but Carl had leverage on his side. He grabbed Randy's right leg and twisted up and over the hull, just enough to tilt Randy's bulk over the side of the boat.

Randy gripped the edges of the frame as he plunged into the water, tilting the boat. Carl stumbled to his knees, trying to gain balance.

Randy reached inside, scrambling to gain purchase on anything he could find. His fingers caught the metal handle of the Coleman lantern and slammed it against the aluminum boat hull. The glow of the lamp swung wide, making the blood on the side of his face look like an oil slick.

"I'm sorry!" Randy reached a free hand toward Carl. "I didn't mean for Tommy to die. It was an accident!"

Carl lashed out, kicking at Randy's hand gripping the boat frame.

Sounds started building. Noises beyond the frantic thrashing of Randy's arms as he tried to get back into the boat. The rush of water. Deep burbling sounds of something rising from beneath the surface.

Randy's eyes grew wide with fear and his shrieks echoed across the water. He struggled frantically to climb into the boat.

Cold droplets rained down on Carl as he fell into the boat on his back. As it happened, he saw the creature explode from the surface of the water. It swung its arms, glistening flaps of pale wrinkled skin and purple veins the color of ripe eggplants.

It thrust up from the muck, parting the water in muddy sheets. Glistening leaves and wildflower buds stuck to its flesh. It swiveled its eyes downward and as Randy twisted to see behind him, he screamed.

The creature opened its maw and peeled mottled, salmon colored lips away from its mouth to reveal rows of discolored fangs. It shook as it opened its mouth, as wide as an oil drum, and descended.

Randy's grip on the boat slid free. He yanked the lantern with him and Carl watched Randy get pulled beneath the murky water. Carl glimpsed his face, open mouthed and screaming in his final moments before the lantern was extinguished.

Carl lay back on the belly of the boat. He stared at the sky and noticed the clouds had cleared. The stars were shining brightly. Everything was quiet.

He was still for a while, waiting for his heart to settle, trying to process the redemption that had happened. He reached for the six pack and opened a beer.

"To you, Tommy." He whispered to the sky overhead. "I love you little brother."

Carl finished the beer and tossing the can aside, reached for the motor.

"Daddy!" Robbie's voice. Happy. A surprise bike trip to come night fishing with him at the lake.

Bubbles rose to the surface of the lake fifteen feet away from the boat . A wide 'v' of a wake began rapidly moving toward the sound of Robbie's voice.

"Robbie, NO! RUN!"

Carl started the motor and gunned it, curling the boat back toward the docks. It was too dark to see the shoreline. All he could do was aim for the other side of the lake. The motor shrieked but Carl wasn't fast enough to keep pace with the creature moving ahead of him.

"ROBBIE!"

Carl drove the boat straight into the bank of the lake, throwing him forward onto the pebble covered shoreline. The motor, buried in the mud, sputtered and died.

Carl stumbled to his feet, searching in the dim light for his son. He ran to the docks. Robbie's bike was there, turned on its side.

He screamed his son's name but there was no answer.

Nothing but quiet darkness.

Carl walked to the end of the dock. The boards shone silver. He felt numb. He looked out over the expanse of the lake and sat down with his legs dangling over the edge of the boards. Beneath him, his shadow danced on the water's surface.

A flood of snapshot memories went through Carl's mind.

Robbie's first day of school. Sleigh riding. Learning to ride his bike. Trick or treating. Christmases. Birthdays. Watching Robbie dance to Led Zeppelin in Winnie the Pooh pajamas. Singing lullabies to him. Heating a bottle of formula. The soft, powdery smell of Robbie's infant skin.

The reflection of the stars rippled on the water of the lake. Carl leaned against one of the dock posts, and lit a cigarette from his pack of Winston's.

After a while, he started singing a lullaby.

And waited.

ABOUT THE AUTHOR

Bob Ford fills his days running an ad agency and considering ripping the phone lines from the wall. He has published various short fiction and has several screenplays floating around in the evil ether of Hollywood. He can confirm that the grass actually is greener on the other side, but it's only because of the bodies buried there. Visit http://coronersreport.blogspot.com to find out what he's currently working on, or if his committal papers to the asylum have been processed.

NIGHT SHIFT AT HOTEL MARA

Dean Harrison

"So how ya likin' the job?"

Eyes studying the various camera angles displayed in the small windows on the computer screen, Bryan Hicks shrugged.

"Kind of boring. You guys ever see any action?"

Chuck Werner snickered around the toothpick dangling beneath his bushy gray mustache. "Nah. We get the occasional drunken disorderly, ya know. But most of the time things are pretty quite. 'Specially here on the nightshift."

Bryan took a sip of the coffee he poured himself from the hotel employee break room and winced. Despite the three packets of sugar and cream, the shit still tasted like melted tire. But at least it was keeping him awake—for now.

"So what's a college boy like you doin' workin' security anyways? Shouldn't you be somewhere makin' the big bucks?"

"It was the only job I could find after failing the police exam." Already Bryan knew he said too much.

"Police exam?" Chuck turned in his swivel chair and looked Bryan up and down. "*You* was gonna be a cop?"

Still watching the screen of camera angles strategically positioned throughout the hotel, Bryan nodded with a thin smile.

"Well...what happened? Wasn't up to snuff?"

With his two friends, guilt and regret knotting up together in his stomach, Bryan rose from the computer terminal and said, "I think I'm going to go patrol the grounds. Been sitting here for too damn long. My ass is getting sore."

Chuck leaned back in his chair and drummed his hands against his pumpkin-size beer belly. "A'ight. Radio if ya need me. We're the only two on duty tonight. And remember, we rotate this here post every forty-five minutes. So don't be too long."

Bryan nodded, thinking, y*eah right, that's why you left me sitting here for two hours while you went on down the street to Paddy's Bar & Grill for you "smoke break", asshole.*

Hooking his radio to his utility belt, Bryan gave chuck a two-finger salute and exited the security booth.

Fucking police exam...and now I'm stuck with this suck-ass *job after busting my ass for four years in college.*

His mother always told him he should've majored journalism—not criminal justice—and become a writer.

His mother told him he wasn't law enforcement material. That he was too sensitive a person and had too kind a heart.

His mother was right.

And she never let him forget it.

Bryan dropped his paper cup of melted tire into a nearby trashcan, waved to Tommy, the check-in clerk, in the front lobby, and made his way down a marble hallway toward the east wing elevators where he saw *her.*

She had a slim hour-glass figure, looked to be about five-foot-four and had a spade-shaped face framed by a long, flowing mane of honey-blonde hair.

There was also a glow about her that drew Bryan in. He couldn't exactly pinpoint what it was, but it turned him on something fierce.

It was against policy for employees of Hotel Mara to fraternize with guests, but—

The woman turned at the sound of his footsteps echoing down the polished corridor. Her eyes were chestnut brown and catlike, her lips full and pouty. She smiled pleasantly as he approached and said, "Hi."

"Evening ma'am," Bryan said, stopping beside her in front of the elevators and patiently waiting for the first of the two gold-plated doors to open.

Her voice was soft, musical, and turned him further on. "Going up?"

"Oh...yes, ma'am."

"Hope there isn't any trouble in the hotel."

Bryan's friendly smile broadened. "No, ma'am. Just have to patrol the floors."

Nodding her head, the woman glanced toward an opening elevator door. "Good to know you'll be watching out for us tonight. Coming with?"

"It's against policy to share elevators with guests. I'll catch the next one."

She flashed an innocent smile and said, "Oh, come on. I won't tell."

A blast furnace roared between his thighs as he struggled *not* to look at the woman's breasts pressing proudly against her beige blouse; he could also plainly see that she wasn't wearing a bra.

"It's silly to wait for another elevator," she continued. "Really, hop aboard. I may need to be escorted to my room. Not feeling very safe. I think I was followed me back to the hotel from the club by a man who wouldn't stop hitting on me. He tried to get me to leave with him, but I managed to get away...I hope."

Despite the ethical side of his brain telling him to be smart, the highly aroused side, which was directly connected to his penis, begged him not to be stupid.

And if she had been followed by some creep and felt she needed a security escort to her room was necessary, then who would it hurt? After all, wasn't it part of his job to look after the guests?

Hell, he could be her hero for the night, and he really liked the thought of that.

So taking a deep breath, Bryan took one hesitant step forward and entered the elevator.

Fuck it, he told himself. *If Chuck can leave the premises and drink while on the clock, then I can walk a pretty lady to her room.*

Suddenly, the ethical side of his brain was in agreement.

She reached over, pressed the button for her floor, and jumped his bones as soon as the elevator doors closed.

With her willowy hands cupping his face, she inserted her tongue into his mouth and moaned deeply with pleasure.

It happened so fast Bryan didn't know how to react.

But his penis did, so he decided to follow its lead whether it got him into trouble or not.

Placing his hands on her small waist, he allowed himself the pleasure of enjoying the long, sensual kiss, and when she finally pulled away, his lips yearned for more.

"Sorry," she said, stepping aside with a slight blush as the elevator ascended. "I don't usually do that kind of thing, believe me. Guess I'm just a sucker for men in uniform."

"It's okay, ma'am," Bryan said, instantly feeling like a jerk as he surreptitiously glanced at the small camera dome in the corner.

"My name's Sarah, by the way. Sarah Sheppard. Since we just shared a kiss, it seems awfully silly for you to call me ma'am. After all, we're probably the same age, um." She eyed his name tag. "Bryan."

The elevator doors parted opened onto her floor. Sarah stepped out and turned around.

"Still walking me to my room?"

Bryan hoped she didn't see his erection throbbing against the front of his navy-blue trousers, but he was almost certain she had.

"Yes m...um...Sarah."

"There you go, Bryan." She winked one lustrous brown eye. "Now you're catching on."

It was Bryan's turn to blush in embarrassment.

Good God, I must look like an idiot to her right now.

But it wasn't like he could do anything about it. And if Chuck saw what happened in the elevator from the security booth—

If he tries to report that, then I'll turn right around and tell management about his slipping out to bars while on duty.

Suddenly, Bryan wasn't so worried about violating his ethics.

And hey, I'm the hero of the day.

Watching the provocative way she moved her hips, his eyes following the movements of her finely-sculpted ass, which was packed tight in her black capris, Bryan followed Sarah to her room, No. 333.

She slipped her keycard into the lock and pushed the door open. "Want to come in?"

Bryan was dumbstruck. "Um...I...I can't—"

Sarah giggled and patted the silver-colored security badge pinned to his pale-blue work shirt.

"You're cute when you're nervous, Bryan," she said. "And I was only kidding. Thanks for the escort. I feel much safer now."

"You're welcome," Bryan said, his blush deepening. "Have a good night."

"I'm sure I will...*now*."

Sarah slipped into her room and gently pushed the door shut without a second glance his way. Bryan interpreted it as an act of mercy.

Turning away from Room 333, he released a hefty sigh and said, "Goddamn."

He knew he would get his balls busted by Chuck when he returned to the booth after making his rounds, but he didn't give a shit.

Roving the rest of the floor to ensure all was kosher, he thought a little more about what happened, and how unlikely it was to have happened.

But hell, it did happen.

And he would never forget it.

Shit...it's on tape!

If he wanted to, he could relive it again and again and again.

When he returned to the security booth Bryan caught Chuck leaning back in his swivel chair, arms folded across his chest, tooth picked clamped between his lips, and eyes clamped shut.

When Bryan swung the door to the booth open and clicked it shut, Chuck woke up, stretched, and scratched his crotch. "Rich bitches safe and sound up there?"

Taking the empty seat in front of the security monitor, Bryan said, "All's quite in Hotel Mara."

"Good," Chuck said, grunting as he stood, hitched up his pants, and exited the booth. "I'm gonna grab a smoke."

Have fun at the bar, Bryan thought, and wondered if it was Chuck who had relentlessly hit on Sarah and followed her back to the hotel.

Watching Chuck wobble toward the front entrance, he muttered, "Wouldn't but it past the fat bastard."

Shaking his head with disgust; Bryan returned his attention to the security monitor, intent on pulling up the video of that incredible elevator kiss with Sarah Sheppard, but instead felt his heart seize with terror by what he saw from a camera angle positioned in one of the east wing elevators.

A long-haired, muscle-bound titan wearing dark sunglass and holding a mean-looking hunting knife lifted a horrified Sarah up into the air, and then choked-slammed her down onto the elevator floor.

"Holy shit," Bryan shouted, watching in disbelief as the man ripped open Sarah's blouse and dug his blade deep into her voluptuous chest, spilling her blood all down her alabaster skin.

Breaking his paralysis, Bryan bolted from the security booth and sprinted for the elevators.

"What's going on?" He heard Tommy yell after him when he passed him in the lobby.

"Call the cops," Bryan shouted back, nearly slipping on the marble floor as he made it to the elevators. "A guest is being...assaulted!"

Vigorously slapping the up-button, he snatched his radio off his belt, called out for Chuck, but received no answer.

"Son-of-a-bitch," he muttered, continuing to beat on the elevator button, not knowing what the hell he was going to do once it came down, if the right one came down, and whether or not it was too late.

What was she doing out of her room? Where was she going? Was that the creep who followed her back from the club? Is it too late to save her?

More than likely, Bryan admitted to himself.

Tommy appeared in the hallway. "I called the police. What's happening, man?"

"There's a guest being attacked with a knife in one of the elevators. God-damned it, come down!"

"You call Chuck?"

"He's not answering his radio."

An elevator dinged. It echoed in the hall. The golden doors to the left opened, revealing an empty car.

"Shit!"

Bryan reached into the empty elevator and hit a random button on the panel to send it back up. Once the doors closed and the car sent on its way, he summoned the other one.

Fear, anxiety, and impatience blossomed in Bryan's gut as he waited for the next elevator to come down.

Tommy was equally as tense, standing rigid by his side, chewing on nervously on his fingernails.

"Hey, did somebody call the cops," said a voice from the front lobby, as a ding punctured the stillness and the elevator doors opened.

Bryan's stomach dropped at the sight before his horrorstricken eyes.

The elevator's empty. No Sarah, no blood, no long-haired Goliath with a knife. Shit...it was the east wing elevators, right?

Yes. He was damn certain. After all, Sarah's room was on the east wing of the hotel.

"Bryan?"

He jumped at the sound of his name. Tommy was looking from him to the elevator and then back as a cop appeared behind him.

"What's the problem here," the cop asked, his voice sounding tired and irritated.

Bryan looked back toward the elevator as its doors began to close. And he could've sworn he heard a distant bout of feminine laughter just as they clamped shut.

"I know what I saw," Bryan insisted to Chuck when he returned from the bar, red-faced and reeking of sour mash whiskey. "She was being stabbed by a man the size of a pro wrestler. He had long, oily brown hair and sunglasses. I'm telling you the truth. He was also wearing—"

"Camera don't lie," Chuck said. "We just rewound the tape. Nothin's there. And there ain't no video of you making out with some broad. See it for yourself. You were alone in that elevator."

Bryan simply shook his head in adamant denial, staring at the security monitor as Chuck, the check-in clerk, and the cop named, Officer Evans, starred at him as if he just stripped down naked before their eyes and did a jig.

"I should arrest you right now just for wasting my time," Evans. "You been drug tested lately?"

"It's just the nightshift," Chuck said. "Sit staring at these cameras long enough and it messes with your head."

"I have to get back to work." Tommy up looked uncertainly at Evans. "Can I go?"

"Yeah, beat it," he said, staring long and hard at Bryan, who dared to return his icy gaze.

"I'm not making this up."

"I should also arrest you for filing a false police report."

"Kid just needs more coffee to wake him up," Chuck chimed in. "All that lack of sleep is makin' him see things."

Bryan assumed Chuck was sticking up for him because of his own indiscretions and the proof thereof, which he didn't really give two shits about.

No, right now, Bryan only cared to prove the soundness of his own sanity.

"Check with Tommy," he said. "Get him to look Sarah Sheppard's name up on the computer. She's in Room 333."

Chewing on another toothpick, Chuck sighed, hitched up his pants, and said, "A'ight. Let's go."

Taking lead from the security booth to the lobby, Bryan tried to get his head around what was happening and found he couldn't.

He didn't hallucinate Sarah, he didn't hallucinate her kiss, and he didn't hallucinate her attack.

All that he knew for certain.

Then what the hell happened to the cameras? Where was the video footage? What the hell was going on?

And the distant, melodic laughter he heard as the elevator doors closed on the empty car—had he imagined it?

At the front desk, Tommy did as requested, ran his fingers along the keyboard of his computer, and said. "There's no guest staying here by that name."

Bryan's stomach dropped. "Try spelling Sheppard with an 'e.' Not an 'a.'"

Tommy did and shook his head apologetically. "Still no."

"Son-of-a-bitch," Bryan whispered, his heart pounding against his ribcage. "But it happened! I walked her to her door for Christ-sake!"

"No you didn't," Evans said. "We watched the footage of that too. You walked *yourself* to the door, and you talked to yourself the entire time."

"I don't believe this," Bryan muttered. "I don't fucking believe *any* of this."

"Go down to the break room," Chuck said, sympathetically. "Get yourself some coffee and take it easy for a bit."

Bryan couldn't help but wonder why Chuck was being so damn understanding.

How could he? None of this made any sense!

Chalking it up to Chuck covering his own ass, Bryan spun around on his heels, took the corner behind the check-in desk and descended the marble steps leading down into the employee break room and the hotel basement.

The break room was vacant, which was a little surprising. Usually someone from housekeeping or engineering was down here reading the newspaper or snoozing at one of the tables crammed into the small room.

Somebody however had recently been here, because there was a pot of coffee freshly brewed by the empty buffet counter.

"Thank God for small favors," Bryan said, pouring himself a cup of coffee and doctoring it up with three packets of sugar and a packet and a half of cream. "Maybe I really did dream it all."

The moment he said it he knew he didn't believe it. That long, warm, sensual kiss was just too real. *Sarah* was just too real.

She *felt* too real. *Tasted* too real.

But there wasn't any video footage of that kiss. Nor was there footage of Sarah's attacker.

And there wasn't any Sarah Sheppard in the hotel. Could she have given him a false name?

It was possible, but it didn't explain the missing video.

Had someone erased it? Doctored it? Was someone playing a cruel prank on him? Was the nightshift and lack of sleep really getting to him, missing with his brain?

Whatever the answer, Bryan felt trapped in an episode of the *Twilight Zone*.

Sitting down at a table, he took a sip of coffee and stared at the bland wall in front of him.

After a minute passed, he was looking through it.

Where did I go wrong? What am I doing here? Why did I choose this path?

Guilt and regret once again entwined together in a tight, tumultuous marriage within the black private hell of his soul.

This wasn't how my life was supposed to be.

He was supposed to be a police officer. He was supposed to be fighting the bad guys. He was supposed to be a hero.

He wasn't supposed to be a lowly security officer stuck in a dead in job that was gradually driving him insane.

And he was pretty sure that's why Laura broke up with him.

Sure, she told him it was because she was planning on going out of state for graduate school next year, and that it would be easier for the both of them to make a clean break now, but Bryan felt that all to be pure bullshit.

She wanted an out and she took it. Now she can go party with all her skanky college friends without this loser hanging around her neck like dead weight.

And that's what he was now—a loser.

Bryan wondered (and not for the first time) what his life would have been like had he gone into print journalism, as his mother had always told him to do.

Maybe he'd be a successful reporter. Maybe he'd still have Laura. Maybe he'd be somebody.

A hero?

All Bryan ever wanted was to be a hero.

Can't do shit about it know.

Could he?

Before he could contemplate that any further, a hysterical bout of laughter echoed in the distance, sending a cold wash of shivers down his back, flooding the chambers of his heart with ice water, causing his thoughts to freeze in his head.

The overhead fluorescents went out, submerging Bryan in darkness.

The laughter came once again.

Bryan's heart hammered rapidly in his chest as he placed his coffee down, stood up from the table, and reached for the flashlight on his utility belt and flicked the switch.

With his other hand, he detached his radio and called for Chuck. "Is the power out up there? Chuck? Are you there?"

The only answer he received was static.

"Shit," he muttered, clipping his radio back on his belt, and throwing the beam on the door from which he came into the break room.

Unable to push back his fear, he hurried to it, gooseflesh nibbling at his arms, and grasped the handle.

It wouldn't turn. The door wouldn't budge.

"What the fuck?"

Was there a lock on the outside? He didn't remember ever seeing one, and either way he didn't have a key for it.

Beating his fist on the door, he shouted out for Chuck, for Tommy, for anyone to come open this fucking door.

But nobody answered his pleas.

The chilling sound of laughter exploded once more.

Bryan spun around and threw the shaky flashlight beam on the opened door across the murky room. All lights were out in the hall beyond the threshold, and there was no sign of life.

There was usually *somebody* down here. The basement was never *completely* vacant.

What the fuck?

"Who was that," he shouted, hoping his fear didn't show in his voice. "You're going to be in a shitload of trouble when I find you!"

After trying the door behind him one last time, he took a deep breath and moved forward with a fragile resolve.

Once in the darkened hall, he peered through the window looking into the darkness filling the main security office to his left and noted the security monitor inside was as well.

He wondered if the elevators on the other side of the basement were out too.

But more importantly he wanted to know who the asshole was playing this absurd joke, which added on to the string of weird shit happening to him tonight.

Who's the mastermind here? Who thinks this shit is funny? Who's ass do I have to kick?

"Bryan?"

Whipping the flashlight beam around, Bryan felt his heart leap in his throat.

Posed seductively with a sly grin in the long white spear of light was Sarah Sheppard. Her thick golden hair spilled down her slender shoulders like silk.

And she was also naked; not a mark of violence or a speck of blood sullying her bosomy torso.

Bryan could only stare stupefied into her big brown eyes beaming with laughter driving a stake of fear into his heart.

"Come Bryan," she said enticingly. "Come meet my father. He's been so looking forward to your visit for some time."

Finding the will to move, Bryan stepped back and nearly jumped from his skin as the door behind him slammed shut him.

"There's no escape," Sarah said. "Silly Bryan. Your fate was sealed the moment you stepped into that elevator with me. Now come! Don't be bashful. We mustn't keep father waiting!"

Bryan's swallowed the ice block of terror stuck in his throat. "What are you?"

Sarah's grin widened. Looking closer, Bryan could see teeth as sharp as tiny knives.

"I'm Delight," she said. "I'm Lust...I'm Thirst...but you already know that, don't you?"

Bryan shook his head, unable to belief what was happening.

This is a dream. This has to be a dream. I fell asleep in the break room. That has to be it. I fell asleep. This is-

"No dream," Sarah finished, extending a willowy hand with talon-tipped fingers. "Come."

And before his terrified eyes, she began change.

⚜

"What do you think is wrong with him," Tommy asked.

Leaning against the check-in counter, Chuck chewed on his toothpick and scanned the empty lobby for hideously misshapen shadows creeping along the wall and scaling the rafters.

Watching...waiting.

Seeing none of those evil monstrosities lingering about, he breathed a deep sigh of relief.

"Like I said before, just tired. You know what twelve hours of pure boredom here can do to ya."

"Yeah, but I've never actually had hallucinations."

"How long you been here again?"

Tommy blinked. "A month."

Chuck pushed away from the counter. "Give it time," he said, walking back to his post without another word.

Bryan was in Hell.

Somehow, at some unknown point in the last hour or so, he had died and descended into Hell.

That was the only explanation for what was happening right before his petrified eyes as Sarah sprouted long leathery wings and tiny moon-shaped horns.

Cold, numbing fear blossomed in Bryan's chest as Sarah's big brown eyes blackened and as an arrow-tipped tail swung to and fro between her skinny legs like a dominatrix's whip.

And when she spoke, her voice was almost reptilian.

"Just down the corridor."

With a ghastly, sharp-toothed grin cracking the once lovely features of her now devilish face, Sarah snatched his wrist, dug her talons into his flesh, and wrenched him forward.

Her grip was sharp and painful.

"Let's us not tarry," she said.

Unable to stop the living nightmare from progressing, Bryan allowed himself to be dragged by the demon-woman with the lovely flow of honey-blonde hair and the perfectly rounded breasts.

Did someone slip something into my coffee while I wasn't looking? Could that explain the crazy shit I'm seeing?

Somewhere along the dark hallway he dropped the flashlight. But that didn't matter, for a door somewhere had opened, and an eerie orange glow spilled into the blackness.

"Do not be afraid, Bryan," said the thing that was Sarah as she led him into the evil light. "Be honored."

Bryan didn't know how the fuck that could be possible.

"Watch your step."

She walked him into the light.

The stench of sulfur immediately struck him in the face as he was led down a spiraling stairwell of polished marble.

"Father," Sarah called out merrily, "*it* is here."

"Called for Bryan to come up and stand guard at the post," Chuck said to Tommy as he headed out the front entrance. "I'm takin' a smoke break."

Without waiting for a response, Chuck stepped out into the nippy night and headed in the direction of Paddy's Bar & Grill.

Of course Bryan wouldn't return, and tomorrow Chuck would have to report to the boys upstairs that he walked off the job without a word to anyone, but that wouldn't be so shocking.

Hotel Mara had a high turnover rate.

Chuck needed a drink badly.

These days alcohol was the only remedy against feelings of guilt, regret, and terror plaguing him every night he worked at Hotel Mara. How he never ended up like all the others who came before him he'd never know. And if only he could find a way to escape it, to break the power of its hold, he'd be out quicker than candle light in a hurricane.

But nearly twenty years had gone by and still here he was, enslaved to the curse of Mara. He'd tried killing himself many times, but the evil would never allow him to go. For whatever reason it needed Chuck, and it made damn sure he knew it too.

Drawing a hefty sigh of resignation, Chuck pushed through the solid oak door of Paddy's Bar & Grill, feeling damn sorry for what was probably happening right now to the unsuspecting Bryan Hicks.

Who stood awestruck as the devil rose from a marble throne.

"His name is Mara," Sarah said, genuflecting before her father, who glowered at them both with eyes as black as onyx.

Bryan felt a warm and wet sensation stream down his legs as he trembled before the ten-foot behemoth looming over him in the sinister glow of the fires rising behind the beast.

"Don't make him angry," Sarah pleaded. "Bow down."

Mara sneered. His teeth were sharp, curved, and salivating. His monstrous visage was heavily bearded and framed by an oily mane of dirty brown hair.

He had four long muscular arms and two massive ram horns. His powerful physique was covered in flesh-colored scales, and as he flexed he unfurled his leathery wings, which were black as the endless night.

"Crawl to me daughter," Mara ordered as he grabbed hold of his stiff yard-long cock, his eyes never leaving Bryan. "And give me your service."

Obediently on hands and knees Sarah crawled to her father, took his erect penis into her mouth, and began to suck on it like a nursing calf.

With one sinewy hand dug into his daughter's hair, Mara sneered at Bryan once again and said, "She's mine." His sneer broadened into a wicked smile. "And so are you."

Behind him, up the long flight of marble stairs, a door slammed shut, and the fires rose higher as lighting crackled throughout the hellish lair.

Mara closed his eyes in ecstasy as he unloaded his seed into Sarah's mouth, and then batted her away like an annoying fruit-fly.

With a whimper, Sarah scampered into a darkened corner of the marble inferno, and folded her wings around her small body like a protective cocoon as she wept.

And with dark, thunderous laughter, Mara stepped forward with one cloven-hoof and reached out for Bryan.

"I am the god of many," he said. "I am the god of seduction...temptation—

Mara grabbed hold of Bryan's throat and squeezed. His sharp talons dug into his flesh, drawing blood as he lifted Bryan from the floor.

—and death!"

Bryan lost consciousness long before he was choke-slammed, and his soul was juiced by the demon that slurped it down like an oyster form its shell.

Chuck tossed back a shot of Evan Williams and savored the hellfire raging down his throat.

Slamming his empty glass down on the chipped surface of the bar, he called out to the barkeep for another as he gazed at his haggard reflection in the dirty mirror across the counter.

Why does it happen? When did it start? And why have I been chosen as supplier?

Those were questions for which he could never find answers, but one thing he knew for sure: he was destined for Hell.

Maybe it was because he himself had given in so easily to temptation. Maybe it was because he had forgone his ethics and allowed let himself be seduced into slavery.

Or maybe it was because, when it came to pussy, demon or not, he was too damn week willed.

Whatever the reason be, Chuck knew he now had a vacant spot to fill on the nightshift; and within the next year another poor soul to sacrifice to the demon who found its home at Hotel Mara.

The barkeep refilled his glass.

"Keep 'em coming," Chuck said, "it's been a helluva night."

ABOUT THE AUTHOR

Dean Harrison is a fan and writer of horror fiction. His first short story, "Chosen Quarry", can be found in the Pill Hill Press anthology "Fem-Fangs". His first novella, "Off Limits", is set to come out February 2011 in the Wicked East Press anthology "Twisted Tales from the Torchlight Inn". Dean resides in his hometown of Mobile, Alabama and is currently working on his first novel.

SANDWALKERS

Michael West

S AND. Sand was the enemy. It gummed up chopper motors, turned fierce war birds into flightless metal hulks. It jammed M-16s, left deadly weapons nothing more than impotent weight, left soldiers defenseless in battle. And, when propelled by Afghanistan's merciless wind, it scoured body armor and skin alike.

Foster wore the same armor and helmet as the Marines he now shadowed through this sandstorm, but he didn't belong to their ranks. The soldiers of Bravo Company knew it the moment they laid eyes on him back at the outpost. They saw his Nikons, saw the hardshell cases for his video gear and his Macbook Pro slung over his shoulders, and their heads wagged. Matching body armor or no matching body armor, journalists stood out like a sore thumb and made easy targets for Taliban snipers.

In previous wars, reporters were viewed as non-combatants, no different from unarmed civilians. Sure, covering the front lines was dangerous work, and of course there were casualties, but they were few and far between. In war, however, things change rapidly, and rarely for the better. Journalists were now viewed as a cog in the American military's propaganda machine, and, as such, they were fair game.

Sand collected around the edges of Foster's ballistic goggles. He pressed his handkerchief firmly against his nose and mouth. The Marines' weapon-mounted lights were now barely visible through the gritty murk ahead.

Foster quickened his pace, tried not to lose sight of the shadowy figure in front of him; the holstered .45 that hung from his belt hammered his hip with each hurried step. He knew these sandstorms could develop without warning, but he'd never seen anything like this. He'd watched dust clouds bubble up, forming a mountain on the horizon—a churning mass that rolled toward Bravo Company like a wave and swallowed them whole.

"Where's this village?" Master Sergeant Conlin yelled, his voice nearly lost to the wind's roar. "We need shelter fast!"

Another voice called out from the veil, "Just ahead, sir!"

Was that Corporal Ross? Yes, had to be. He was on point.

In moments, structures loomed out of the sand like a gothic citadel. The

Marines hugged a stone wall, preceded with caution; they didn't expect to dodge sniper fire in this storm, just as they didn't expect the town elders to form a welcoming committee, but they weren't taking any chances.

Wooden poles materialized—a framework for awnings. Tarps, ripped from their moorings, now flapped in the gale like tattered flags. Foster noticed they were not traditional Afghan colors. No. They were red and white, the motif of Arab insurgents.

Corporal Ross noticed it too. He ducked beneath these tarps and swept their path with his eyes, leveling the barrel of his M2. Nicknamed "Ma Deuce," the heavy machine gun was his best friend in-theater. He found a locked entrance and motioned them forward.

"McBride," Conlin called. "You're up!"

Private McBride spoke both major Afghan languages: Dari and Pashto. He put his gun aside and knocked on the door, shouting greetings in both tongues.

No response.

"Try Arabic!" Corporal Miller chimed in. His eyes moved from those tattered tarps to Conlin. "Want me to break it down, Sarge?"

"Move on," Conlin ordered. "Look sharp, people!"

The Marines resumed their march. They strode single file, weapon-mounted lights illuminating their immediate surroundings and little else. The opposite side of the street was a specter in the sand.

As they moved deeper into the village, Foster was reminded of a Wild West ghost town. Wind howled between scattered brick structures, buffeting Bravo Company with grit and bits of trash. An old-fashioned motorcycle lay riderless on its side in the dirt street. A propane tank sat on one end of a vendor's make-shift scale, but the other side, now full of sand, weighed more. A metal sign rattled with every gust. But there were no goats, no dogs, and no people. No signs of life at—

"Jesus!" Miller called out. "Would you look at this shit?"

Foster glanced over and saw the severed head of a camel. It was tied to a post along their walkway, swinging in the wind like a piñata. Blood dripped from its ragged stump, splattering dirty steps below. Its eyes were wide, and its tongue hung out like a wolf in one of those old Tex Avery cartoons.

"Sick fucks," Miller concluded, his eyes locked with the animal's glassy stare. "Probably the village elder's ride. Cock-suckers cut off its head as a warning."

"Wound's too jagged," Corporal Harrison corrected. Bravo Company's medic approached with care, sensing a possible trap; his eyes darted between this mutilation and the sandy void beyond. He touched the bloodied stump with his gun barrel, spun it around to get a better look. "This baby was ripped off, not cut off."

Foster reached for his Nikon and snapped a quick photo. Soldiers spun instinctively toward the flash. Miller aimed his rifle squarely at Foster's chest. The journalist lifted his hands in surrender, the Nikon swinging from his neck on its strap.

Miller glared at him. "Fuckin' shutter bug."

"Save it," Conlin snapped. "Let's move."

"Sure thing, Sarge." Miller backed away, but his weapon never lowered.

Foster hesitated, then followed along with his companions, feeling more isolated, more alone, than ever before. The wind whistled its happy tune, taunting him. He glanced back over his shoulder and saw that the post had already been swallowed up by the blowing sand, taking the bloody camel head with it.

Ross slowed as another entrance came into view; he nodded to his right and McBride moved quickly to flank him. Conlin crouched at the door; the knob turned easily and a gust of wind pushed it in.

McBride shouted bilingual greetings, waited, then said, "Nobody's home."

"Nobody's answering. There's a difference." Conlin peered into silent darkness, then eased out of the way and motioned Ross forward.

The corporal stepped in, "Ma Deuce" preceding him through the door. He illuminated every dark corner, eyes and weapon moving in unison, trigger finger ready. Nothing rose up out of the shadows to challenge him, however.

"Clear!"

Conlin led them into shelter. McBride and Harrison were right behind him. Foster was last, accompanied by Miller who closed and bolted the door behind them, blocking out the wind.

In the glow of their Surefire lights, Foster saw evidence of a struggle. Chairs and tables overturned. Ceramic bowls strewn over dusty floorboards, some already shattered, others breaking beneath the soldier's boots. And, most disconcerting, dark stains on the walls. Foster didn't need to be a medic to know they were dried blood.

McBride saw it too. "Merry fuckin' Christmas."

Foster nodded, surprised that he'd nearly forgotten the date. That was the angle of his piece, after all: how these men coped with being separated from their families during the holidays. Now, he didn't know what his story was.

If the others noticed the blood and shambles, they gave no indication. Miller remained on guard by the door with his shouldered M-16. Ross stationed himself on the opposite end of the mess, "Ma Deuce" still at the ready; his hulking frame filled a darkened archway that led to the next room. Harrison flanked him, his eyes on Conlin, waiting for orders; he didn't have to wait long.

"Don't get comfortable, people," the master sergeant cautioned. "Give me a sweep. If there's so much as a flea in this motherfucker, I wanna know."

They went into the next room, the Marines' movements as choreographed and precise as a ballet, though Foster thought these battle-hardened warriors might take offense at the comparison. Foster's gaze darted left then right, following the lights projected from their weapons and wishing for his own set of night-vision goggles. There wasn't much to find in this modest dwelling, and what little there was had been ransacked. A few pictures hung on the walls, their glass cracked, their frames askew. Long pillows were scattered about, torn open and bleeding stuffing. Hand-woven rugs that once covered the wooden floor lay bunched up to one side, as if something had been dragged across them. And, of course, there was more blood; it decorated the walls like modern art and streaked the naked floorboards.

There had been a massacre here. That much was clear. But there were no bodies. No bullet holes. No signs of explosives or—

Ross held up his hand.

The Marines stopped, listened.

And then Foster heard it too. Rapid breathing. At first, he thought it was the sound of his own nervous respiration, but no. They were not alone in the room.

The soldiers whirled around, their lights spearing a floral-printed sheet that hung on the far wall. Ross pointed, took a step toward it. McBride nodded, covering him.

Foster felt his entire body tense. Writers had active imaginations, and right now, his was feeding him every conceivable horror that might be lurking behind that curtain. His hand left his Nikon, traveled down to his belt; he popped the snap on his holster, ready to draw his .45 with the speed of a gunslinger.

Ross reached out, curled his fingers around the edge of the curtain, and then yanked it aside.

Two Afghan children cowered from the light, a girl and a boy. They were filthy, emaciated, their eyes just as wide and staring as the camel's that hung outside, but they were alive. The girl was a teenager, covered in a long, brightly colored dress that was now smudged and torn. Dark hair trailed from beneath her tattered head scarf, hiding half her face. Tears had cleared lines in the dirt on her exposed cheek. The boy was much younger, perhaps six or seven, and his once white clothes were covered in so much blood that they now appeared tie-dyed in the light.

The girl held up her hands and said two words in perfect English.

"Don't shoot."

Outside, the wind roared and howled like an animal. It hammered the stone walls with dirt and sand, creating a sound akin to frenzied scratching. And it pushed on the door, demanding to be let in, whining its frustration through the cracks.

Foster righted an overturned chair and sat down. He emptied sand and pebbles from his boots, watching the Marines, who were intent on their duties. Ross and Miller stood sentry, weapons still at the ready, refusing to stand down even though the building had been cleared. Conlin sat at a nearby table with his handheld radio, searched for an active frequency, but so far, only found static. Across the room, McBride and Harrison put their guns aside and bent down to work with the children.

The girl poured out her frantic tale in Dari or Pashto, but "don't shoot" appeared to be the only English she knew.

Foster found that sad.

The boy hadn't uttered a word in any language. He sat with his chin on his knees and stared blankly off into space, a blood pressure cuff wrapped firmly around his filthy arm. Harrison modified it to fit the boy's smaller limb, and Foster could tell this wasn't the first time the medic had checked a child's vitals.

Conlin looked up from his radio, frustrated. "What's she saying over there, Private?"

"She's in shock, Sarge," McBride told him.

"If I wanted her medical condition, I'd ask Harrison. I need to know what the hell happened here."

"She..." The private stood, frowned. "She says it was Sandwalkers."

Conlin blinked at him.

At the door, Miller burst out laughing and shook his head in disbelief.

"First," McBride continued, "they got the goats, got the horses and the camels, then they came back for the villagers."

Foster's eyes darted between the three men. "What's a 'Sandwalker?'"

"It's bullshit, Shutter Bug," Miller answered with his usual eloquence. "A fuckin' fairytale."

McBride shrugged and gave a more helpful, albeit less believable response, "It's another name for a Manticore, like a...a distant cousin to the Sphinx: body of a lion, bat wings, with a man's face and a scorpion's tail."

Miller chuckled and cracked, "Sounds like the date Harrison took to prom."

No one else laughed.

But it *was* ridiculous, the very idea that this carnage was the result of a rampage by mythical desert chimeras. Some insecure part of Foster's mind even considered that it might all be a joke the Marines were playing on him. After all, none of them were crazy about having a journalist tag along. And Marines all stuck together, didn't they? Semper Fi, and all that?

Conlin scowled as if he'd somehow heard Foster's thoughts. "All right, people. Obviously, the girl's seen some traumatic shit."

"I think they both have." Harrison removed the blood pressure cuff and packed up his gear. "They're also hot, hungry, and dehydrated, which is a good cocktail for hallucinations."

The master sergeant gave a disappointed nod; he took his hands off the radio, surveyed the faces of his men. "Okay, here's the facts. We've got to assume that whoever did this is still in the area. We're cut off, and we won't be able to establish a satellite link until this storm dies down. Even if we could, no chopper's gonna swoop down and extract us, and no predator drone's gonna give us any useful intel, not in this shit. So we've got to do what we do best...watch each other's backs." He took a pack of cigarettes from his breast pocket and slid one between his lips; it bobbed up and down as he spoke. "That's the bad news."

"What's the good news?" Foster asked, unnerved.

"The good news?" Conlin lit up, inhaled deeply, then exhaled like a steam engine ready to blow; the smoke swirled around his helmet, glowing in the weapon-mounted lights like a halo. "For the moment, the building's secure, and the storm should pin the bad guys down the same way we're pinned down." He pointed at Foster with his smoldering cigarette, emphasizing every word. "They can't *hit* us if they can't get *to* us."

Foster nodded. Looking at the children, however, at the blood they'd bathed in, he felt little comfort, even in this tight knot of well-armed warriors. "How long do sandstorms usually last?"

"Depends."

"On what?"

Conlin blew more smoke. "On if it's a *Haboob* or a *Shamal*."

"What's the difference?"

"*Haboobs* die down in a few hours. *Shamals* can go on for days."

The Afghan girl tugged on McBride's uniform and started in again. Her eyes were not as manic as they had been before, but they were no less haunted. In fact, she seemed quite anxious about something.

"What's she going on about, Private?" Conlin wanted to know.

McBride held up his hand, listening to the girl's harried rambling, making certain he heard every nuance and his translation was accurate. "She says that we can't stay here. She says it's not safe."

"No shit," Ross growled softly, his powerful machine gun cradled in his muscular arms.

"If we don't leave right now," McBride continued, "the Sandwalkers will kill us the same way they killed her parents and her other brothers and sisters."

"You and your brother have got nothin' to worry about, little lady." Miller stepped forward, smiled confidently. "Me and my squad here have fought monsters before, and this..." He presented his M-16; the barrel was pointed away from her, but she recoiled against the back of the chair as if squarely in its crosshairs. "...will put their dicks in the dirt before they can even lay a hand on you."

Realizing she couldn't understand a word of it, he glanced up at McBride.

"Go on, tell her not to worry. Tell her she dances with total fucking bad-asses."

The private almost certainly paraphrased, but the girl seemed to grasp the sentiment, even if she didn't find it as reassuring as Miller intended. She relaxed a bit in her chair and hugged her brother to her side, combing his disheveled hair with her fingers. Her troubled eyes drifted slowly to the door and never left.

Foster's Swedish grandmother once told him that the Sandman was a diminutive creature in a very long nightcap, a helpful little sprite that carried a huge sack full of magic sand over his tiny shoulder. If you were good all day long, so her story went, the Sandman crept into your room late at night and sprinkled some of that sand into your eyes. This was supposed to put you into a deep, untroubled slumber where nothing awaited you but the most pleasant and wonderful of dreams.

It was an innocent fairy tale, told with love and affection, but even as a child, Foster found it all quite sinister. He'd have nightmares about a horrible little troll who snuck into his bed at night, cackling as it emptied its entire sack over his face until he suffocated beneath the weight of a huge mound of sand. And when he awoke, Foster found grit still lodged in the corners of his eyes, evidence that he was lucky to have survived to see another dawn.

Now, as he watched these Afghan children drift off to sleep, their angelic faces covered over in blood and very real sand, Foster was reminded of innocence corrupted. And as he looked over at Conlin and McBride, napping in chairs with their helmets pulled down over their faces, he thought of the horrors witnessed by an entire generation of young men and women, and he wondered if any of them would ever have pleasant dreams again.

Harrison plucked a deck of cards from his pocket and invited Foster to a friendly game of poker. The journalist was eager to oblige. He welcomed any distraction from these blood-stained walls, from the incessant drone of that damned wind outside.

"You have any family back home, Corporal?" Foster asked.

The medic shuffled his deck. "This for your story?"

Foster blinked. "Just making small talk."

Harrison dealt cards and said, "I've got a wife and a six-year-old boy. She was supposed to buy him this remote control Iron Man figure for Christmas. She wanted to say it was from Santa, but I told her, 'Hell no! You put "From Daddy" on that one!'" He chuckled ruefully, then glanced at his watch and considered the time difference. "He's probably opened it by now. I can't wait to see the pictures."

The journalist fanned out his cards without looking at them. "Must suck, missing out on so much?"

From the doorway where he still stood watch with Ross, Miller sneered. "Do they actually teach a class in stupid questions at journalism school?"

"What's your problem, Miller? I'm here to tell *your* story, to help you—"

"Bullshit!" the corporal spat, then he looked over at the sleeping Afghan children and lowered his voice. "You're here to *steal* our story and make it yours, to help nobody but yourself. See, I know all about you."

"Is that so? Enlighten me."

"A Marine's on trial right now for fucking war crimes because of pricks like you," Miller accused. "He finished off some wounded asshole down in Fallujah, some insurgent that had been killin' his friends all day long, and if the tables were turned, would've drug him off and decapitated him live on the fucking web. Was he the only one to do it? Hell no. He was just the only sorry sonofabitch to get caught on tape."

The corporal pointed at his own helmet.

"And you people...do you even take a second to *think* about the effect a video like that's gonna have? Hell no! All you think about is your fucking ratings and the fact that you just got the scoop on everybody else. Now, that crap's all over the damn net for any suicide bomber to see and *we're* the ones here with targets on our backs." Miller sounded more frustrated than angry now; he sat at the table across from them and placed the butt of his M-16 against the wood. "So, while we're fighting these fuckers the best way we know how, you're taking pictures for the enemy's recruitment posters. *That's* my problem."

"I see." Foster gave a single, slow nod. "Well, I don't pretend to know anything about you, Miller, but..." He pointed to the Afghan girl. "...I saw the way you acted with her, and I got the feeling that you might actually be an okay guy."

Harrison smiled into his cards before he caught himself, but Miller didn't notice. Miller's eyes were locked with Foster's.

"And when you told her that you fought monsters, I actually believed you," the journalist said, and he meant it. "I believed you because you're right; anybody who kills men, women, and children for shock value is about as evil a creature as I can think of. *My* problem is that terrorists don't have a monopoly on evil. See, in my world, monsters don't just come in one shape, size, religion, or uniform. So, you fight them your way..." He nodded at Miller's M-16, then held up his Nikon. "...and I'll fight them mine. But, since neither one of *us* is a monster, there should be no reason why we can't do our jobs without pissing in each other's canteens."

They regarded each other for a moment, neither one blinking.

Harrison spoke up, anxious to change the subject. "So are we going to play poker, or what?"

"You guys can play if you want to," Miller told them. "I got work to do."

And with that, the corporal stood and took up his position at the door.

Harrison leaned across the table as if to share a secret. "Don't let Miller get to you. He's a little more gung-ho than some, but I trust him with my life, and so should you."

"I trust all of you." Foster shifted in his chair. "And before this is over, I hope you'll trust me."

Miller eyed the journalist with skepticism. "We'll see how you do in a fire fight. If it comes to—"

"Quiet," Ross called out, and their eyes shot to him. "Listen!"

Miller cocked his head to the left for a moment, then shrugged. "I don't hear anything."

Ross nodded. "Exactly."

And then it hit them all in the same instant.

The winds had stopped.

Silence met Conlin's preliminary requests for evac, but the sergeant kept at it, and in time, his determination was rewarded with a static-laced female voice. "Move... four...the terrain to...extraction."

"Say again?...all after 'move?'"

She repeated, much clearer this time. "Move approximately four kilometers farther up the terrain to a hilltop for dawn extraction. Over."

"Copy that. Bravo Company over and out." Conlin holstered his radio, stood and pointed to the sleeping children. "McBride, explain it to 'em."

The private gave a quick salute and obediently crossed the room. When he nudged the Afghan girl, her eyes snapped open and she recoiled into her chair with a guttural moan. McBride held his up his hands as if to surrender, then spoke a few soft words. Whatever they were, she nodded her agreement, then woke her brother and repeated them to him.

"Ross," Conlin called, but his eyes were on the door. "You're on point. And Miller—"

"Rear guard, yes sir." The corporal smiled. "Don't worry, top, I got your back."

"Then let's move."

"What about me?" Foster asked, feeling invisible again.

"What about you?" the sergeant responded.

"Is there something I can do?"

"You can keep up."

A thud. Foster flinched, looked up. Dust rained and stray bits of leaves and reeds drifted down from the thatched ceiling.

Something landed on the roof.

"What the fuck?" Miller wanted to know, his voice hushed, the barrel of his M-16 aimed at the rafters.

The Afghan girl shrieked. She scooped up her brother, took off for the far corner of the room and hunkered down, tried to make herself as small as possible. Her brother's arms were locked around her neck, his face buried in her tattered headscarf; he sobbed and called out words that made no sense to Foster's ears.

From the roof came an answering cry; a symphony warming up—brass and woodwind sections playing different songs at the same time. It was as deafening as it was alien.

McBride ran after the children and whatever was on the roof moved with him. Foster heard it shift, heard it claw at the surface coating of plastered straw. And the wooden rafters cracked beneath the excess weight, cracked right above McBride's head.

"Look out!" Foster called.

McBride flashed his light around just as the flimsy ceiling collapsed. Splintered beams struck him square in his helmet. He went down hard, buried beneath split slats and reeds, beneath leaves and mud, beneath.

Foster staggered back wide-eyed, unable to believe what he saw.

Perched atop the debris was a winged nightmare. It landed on all fours in a supportive crouch like a cat. A very *big* cat. Leathery wings spread wide, flapped, and then folded neatly over its hunched back. It paused—red, malignant eyes glaring; bits of the roof still stuck in its dark, unkempt mane—and then it took a step toward the Afghan children with one menacing talon. Its tail swung behind it, flogging fallen rafters; not a lion's tail, Foster noticed, but the segmented appendage of a scorpion.

The journalist stood there, one hand on his camera and the other on his gun, poised to shoot the thing one way or the other, yet unable to move. Beside him was Conlin. The sergeant had no doubt seen much in his tours of duty, but it was obvious that he'd never seen anything like this.

"Real," he muttered aloud, his voice low and hoarse. "God...*damn.*"

The Manticore took another step forward, smooth muscles flexing beneath its pelt, membranous wings fluttering. Its tail now stood erect, swaying back and forth like a cobra ready to strike; there was something at the tip of it, something razor sharp that gleamed in the lights. Those red eyes narrowed and its lips parted with a silky purr, revealing rows of triangular teeth. Shark's teeth.

Miller bared his own teeth and uttered a snarl of primal anger. He thrust the barrel of his M-16 toward the thing and opened fire. Flowers of blood bloomed and wilted across the creature's side in rapid succession. Its purring turned to a loud, cacophonous screech that once more reminded Foster of a symphony in need of a conductor.

The Manticore spread its wings and flapped them, fanning dust and debris. Foster couldn't tell if it were attempting to take flight or simply trying to shield itself from Miller's projectiles. It succeeded in neither.

At that point, Ross stepped forward, opened up with "Ma Deuce," and it was all over. Massive shells reduced the creature's head to shrapnel. The Manticore collapsed on a death bed of fallen roofing, tattered wings enfolding its corpse like a bloody shroud.

Harrison pushed past them. He slung his rifle, knelt at the rubble, and dug frantically for McBride. Miller followed his lead, glancing up through the jagged hole in the ceiling with increasing regularity, clearly waiting for more creatures to poke their heads through.

Another thud on the roof, this time over the back room where they'd found the children. Foster flinched and spun toward the darkened archway. Ross took aim. From his kneeling position, Miller joined him. Harrison paid no notice and kept right on burrowing with his hands.

A hand slapped Foster's back. Conlin. "Get 'em," he shouted and pointed.

Foster ran to the Afghans. He grabbed the girl by her elbow and pulled her up to her feet. She drew away, clutching her brother tightly to her breast, dampening his hair with her tears.

"It's okay," the journalist said. He wrapped his arm around her waist and shoveled her across the room. "We're going to be all right." He knew she didn't understand a word of it, but he said it anyway. Perhaps he just needed to hear it himself.

"Marines," Conlin called as he backed away, aiming his rifle past Foster and into the dark.

"We're not leavin' a man behind, Sarge," Miller replied, covering Harrison. The medic continued to dig.

In the next room, the roof gave way. Sounds of splintering boards joined that horrible symphony of a Manticore cry. The thing was inside.

"Got him," Harrison announced. He pulled an arm from the debris, gave it a tug, then turned to Miller. "Help me!"

Keeping his M-16 on the archway, Miller reached down with one hand, grabbed a fistful of McBride's uniform and helped yank his comrade free.

Conlin nodded in relief. "Is he—?"

"He's alive, Sarge," Harrison said, two fingers on McBride's neck. Then they dragged his unconscious body across the floor, backed rapidly toward the entrance; Harrison used both hands while Miller's right arm still held the rifle. Then the Manticore pounced on them.

Foster never heard it make a sound, and its speed was incredible. It seemed to materialize in mid leap. Its fur was a maroon blur in the lights, the same color as dried blood, and its teeth were white as Christmas snow.

Miller instinctively pulled his trigger, but by then the thing's jaws had closed around McBride's torso and it wrenched the body from their grasps. Wings fanned out and flapped, and the thing swooped up through the hole in the ceiling its twin had made with McBride still in its mouth. Its long, segmented scorpion's tail snaked through the air like a streamer and was gone.

"McBride!" Miller screamed, and then he fired another futile volley of shells into the night sky. "Motherfuckers!"

Sergeant Conlin turned his attention to the entrance, fumbled with the knob. The door was barely open a crack when two sets of talons pushed through. Foster's heart stopped, and in his arms, the Afghan girl screamed.

Ross muttered a curse and spun toward the door just as the creature wedged it open and slammed Conlin against the wall. The corporal pulled his trigger and unleashed Hell, sending the thing's shattered skull flying backward, fountaining blood. Their path was now clear.

The sergeant stumbled to his feet and managed to get enough wind back in his lungs to yell commands, "Let's go, people! Go now! Go, go, go!"

They ran out into the night.

Ross sprinted up the walkway, "Ma Deuce" laying down an uninterrupted field of fire. Foster and the Afghan children hadn't even cleared the doorway before he'd cut down another beast with his shells. He pivoted left, then right, searching for his next target. There was a screeching roar as it found him instead.

The Manticore charged out from an alley; it leapt on Ross' back and knocked him off the walk. He landed face-first in the sand, the creature straddling him. Ross didn't scream or call out in any way. He didn't have the time. The beast decapitated him with its jaws, then spit his helmeted head into the street like a peach pit.

Miller walked toward the Manticore with his M-16, casually firing as he moved. Blood splattered from its body and it let out a shriek that rang through Foster's skull like cathedral bells. It hopped off Ross' spurting corpse, spread its wings and soared.

Behind them, another Manticore leapt at Corporal Harrison. The creature's tail whipped around, and its knife-like tip skidded across his chest armor in a burst of sparks. The corporal drew his rifle, but before he could fire off a shot, the stinger lashed out again and buried itself in his face, cleaving his skull in two. He was lifted off the walkway and flung aside.

Jesus! Foster's mind cried, as if the word were magic, as if uttering it on this night would make all these horrible visions go away. *They're everywhere! How many can there be?*

The Manticore pounced on what remained of Harrison, who'd been good with children and wanted nothing more than to see pictures of his own son's Christmas joy. Wings extended from its lean body and it took triumphant flight, its kill dangling from between its pointed teeth. Blood fell like hot rain as it passed overhead, sprinkling the walkway and the sandy street beyond.

All this happened in the space of a minute. Then Conlin plucked the radio from his vest and screamed into it. "Dust Off Fifteen, we have a nine-line in progress!"

Foster pressed himself flat against the stone wall, still holding the sobbing Afghan girl around the waist. He suddenly realized that he didn't even know her name. Her brother let go of her neck and clamped his hands over his tiny ears, trying to block out the sounds of Miller's gunfire.

In front of them, Conlin was still on the radio, relaying their location, their casualties, and stressing that a firefight was in progress. He did not, however, share any details about *what* they were fighting. Something sharp burst from his throat in a glut of blood, spearing his radio and ending the conversation—a Manticore stinger, driven straight through his neck from behind.

The beast turned its attention to Foster and the children. It glared at them, narrow red eyes burning with hunger. And when it flicked its tail, Conlin's head came unhinged from his falling body.

Foster instinctively reached for his camera; it came to whirring life in his hands, creating a rapid *click-click-click* and a series of brilliant flashes. In that harsh, artificial light, he got his first good look at the Manticore's hideous face. The myth claimed it to be that of a man, but nothing could've been further from the truth. The nose was triangular, flat and flayed, bat-like, and its skin was as dark and wrinkled as a raisin.

Blinded, the Manticore screeched and turned away, turned right into Miller's line of fire.

"Eat shit, Fuckface!" the corporal shouted, pulling back on his trigger.

A volley of shells opened that horrid face. One of the creature's eyes exploded and it rolled off the walkway, collapsed in the sand, blood spreading out from beneath its body in a dark, viscous pool. Another Manticore swooped down and grabbed it up. Perhaps they were cannibalistic, or maybe they had their own rule about never leaving a comrade behind.

Foster scanned the walkway and the street beyond. Sergeant Conlin's body was gone as well. So were Ross and the other dead Manticore. Puddles, streaks, and splatters of blood were the only evidence that they had ever existed at all.

<hr />

Miller sat on the edge of the walkway, staring out across the sand toward the rising sun. "When that chopper comes, you get the kids outta here."

"What about you?"

The corporal answered Foster's question with a question. "Why'd those things bug out of here so fast?"

"I don't know." And he didn't care. They'd left them alone, left them alive. That was enough. "Animals can sense things people can't. Maybe they can hear the chopper coming, maybe they think it's bringing reinforcements."

"Or maybe they knew it was dawn."

Foster shrugged. "Maybe."

"They all flew off in that direction." Miller nodded at the mountains on the horizon. "There's caves up there, miles of 'em. Dark places where they can hide from the wind and the sun, maybe even from God Himself. Anyway, it's just an educated guess, but I gotta start somewhere."

Foster gaped at him. "You're not going after them?"

"Somebody has to."

"By yourself? That's crazy!"

"I don't expect you to understand."

"Good, because I don't." Foster held up his Nikon. "I've got pictures, Miller. Proof. Like you said, we shoot this stuff, put it on the web, and it goes viral. When they see these things, they'll have to—"

"You fight the monsters your way, and I'll fight them mine." Miller gave his rifle a loving pat, as if it were his faithful dog, then he lifted his gaze to meet Foster's unbelieving stare. "They were my family, Shutter. The only one I've ever had. I owe it to 'em, to *their* families, to find 'em and bring 'em home."

The journalist opened his mouth to say something else, anything that would dissuade Miller from this insanity. And then a terrible, insufferable picture developed in his mind. Harrison's wife and six-year-old boy, standing over an open grave, over an empty casket, never knowing where the man they loved had gone, never having the chance to say good-bye.

Foster shook his head, denying the image. He stepped off the walk, stood for a moment in the hot desert sun, then shaded his eyes with his hands. "You'll die out here."

The corporal shrugged. "Marines die every day, Shutter." He stroked the barrel of his M-16. "But before I go, I'm takin' the rest of those bastards with me." For a moment, he looked solemn—resigned to his fate, then he stood, smiled down at the journalist and said, "Don't you have to go write your story now?"

Foster shook his head and slowly backed away. "Their story, not mine."

"You know, Shutter," Miller chuckled, "I've got the feeling you might actually be an okay guy."

The corporal turned, stepped inside the open doorway, and kept out of sight.

Morning skies purred with powerful rotors. A Blackhawk helicopter. As Foster watched its sleek silhouette descend, exhaust blurring the bright orange dawn, he understood how the chopper earned its name. It swooped down just outside the village, landed with its twin engines still running, and waited.

The journalist relaxed a little, but not completely. He wouldn't relax completely until he was back at the fortified base, perhaps not even then. He looked over his shoulder.

The Afghan girl swayed on her feet, clearly exhausted, but still managing to hold onto her sleeping brother. Foster reached out and pried the boy from her arms. She didn't want to give him up at first, but the journalist smiled at her, let her know that everything was going to be fine now, and she offered a tentative grin of thanks in return.

Together, they hurried to the waiting chopper and never looked back.

From the shadows, Miller watched them go, then he glanced down at the weapon in his hands.

"This is my rifle," the corporal said aloud. "There are many like it, but this one is mine."

He took the handkerchief from around his neck and wiped the barrel.

"I will keep my rifle clean and ready, even as I am clean and ready. We will become part of each other."

When the sound of rotors faded, he stepped out onto the walkway and turned his eyes back to the desert, to the distant mountains beyond.

"Before God, I swear this creed. My rifle and I are the defenders of my country. We are the masters of our enemy. We are the saviors of our life."

He upended his canteen against his lips, drained it dry, then tossed it aside.

"So be it, until victory is America's and there is no more enemy."

Miller leveled his M-16 and walked out across the sand.

ABOUT THE AUTHOR

Michael West is a member of the Horror Writers Association and served as President of its local chapter, Indiana Horror Writers. He lives and works in the Indianapolis area with his wife, their two children, their bird, Rodan, and turtle, Gamera. His children are convinced that spirits move through the woods near their home.

SPLINTERS

Adam P. Lewis

Sam hoisted the axe over his head and swung it down into the dried bark of a barren pine tree. The axe blade split into the trunk scattering splinters about the ground. Sam wiggled the axe head free and lifted it and swung it over his shoulders, bearing the blade into the trunk once again. This time, the axe head crashed through the trunk, creating a large gash in the side of the pine tree.

Sam pressed his middle and forefingers together and made the Sign of the Cross across his chest. He pleaded, "I beg of you, Lord, don't let me find another."

Sam's arms shook as he freed the axe head from the tree. His knees began to knock and the hairs on the nape of his neck stood on end. His skin turned cold as he cautiously bent down and peered into the hollow of the tree. His eyes widened as they affixed on what he found inside.

"Mother of God!" Sam yelled, jumping back away from the tree.

He sprinted down mountainside. The momentum of running down the steep slope carried him faster than his legs could move underneath him. He nearly lost his balance, but caught his footing many times until a tree root protruding from the ground hooked his foot, causing him to stumble head over heels down the slope, with his axe still in hand. The blade nicked his arms, legs, and cheeks and came within inches from gouging his neck and abdomen and eviscerating him—by axe.

He regained his legs and stood and started sidestepping down the mountain. His feet slid on loosened dirt and rocks as he pressed the axe head into the ground behind him, using it for leverage. When he reached the bottom of the slope, he ran past his fellow lumberjacks yelling, "Mr. Foreman…Mr. Foreman!"

The lumberjacks were all on edge. The slightest yell of the foreman's name caught their attention. They all stopped chopping and sawing and turned their heads to Sam. Upon seeing the expression on his face they all knew another was found. The expression was fear. They've seen it plastered across other lumberjacks' faces and felt it upon their own.

"Mr. Foreman…Mr. Foreman!" Sam continued yelling as he approached his boss.

The foreman sighed loudly and slammed a flat palm on his topography map.

He yelled over his shoulder, "For Christ's sakes! We're behind schedule. What the hell's the problem now?"

Winded from the sprint down the slope, Sam explained between deep inhales, "There's another one. I found it while I was clearing dead trees like you ordered. My axe chopped clean through the bark and into the hollow of a pine. I freed it and looked inside. And that's when I saw—I found—I found another one!"

"Dammit," the foreman slammed his hand on the map again. The hard surface of a fallen tree underneath the map sent a stinging sensation through his wrist and up his arm. He shook the pain away, picked up his axe and pointed it up the hill. "Go on now an' show me where."

Sam led the foreman the slope. Behind them, the entire lumberjack crew followed. Each carried their axes in front of them in protective stances, ready to thrust their blades into anything that attacked them. As the hiked, they scanned the forest. Their eyes darted back and forth, peering into the negative spaces between trees and shrubs. With each swish of breeze fluttering tree limbs, their nerves caused them to flinch and tighten their grips on heir axe handles.

When they reached the hollowed out pine, the foreman bend down and peered inside. When his eyes caught sight of what was inside, the axe handle tightened within his grasp, turning his knuckles white with anger. He stepped back away from the tree and pointed to Sam, "Yous found him, yous cut him out!"

Sam's voice trembled. "Yes, Mr. Foreman."

"And yous there," the foreman said, pointing to Steve, " yous help him. I want that tree there cut down. Then I want yous two to remove Glen's body an' bury 'im."

Steve swallowed hard. "Not me, Mr. Foreman."

"What did yous just say?" Shocked that an employee refused to do as ordered, the foreman grinded his teeth loud enough for everyone gathered around to hear.

Steve's voice trembled. He found the foreman intimidating. He was tall, bearded and had a mean disposition. He was also strong; enough to fight any man or any animal for that matter. It was rumored that the foreman saved three men from being killed and eaten by a grizzly bear ten years earlier. The foreman's choice of weapon to bring down the bear was a dull axe. Around his neck, he wore a necklace with the grizzly's nails hanging off a piece of leather, a trophy that fueled the legend.

"I said not me, Mr. Foreman. I've got twin three-month-olds at home and a good wife. I'm quitting before I'm next. Anyone of us could be next. I'm no good to my family dead. I can find lumber work elsewhere on a mountain that's safe."

The foreman shook his head in disbelief. "Yous want to run then fine, go on an' run. But ya have to make yous way down the mountain alone and without that there axe. It's property of Byrne Paper. Leave it behind."

Steve's grip on the axe hardened. He didn't want to let it go. He knew it was all that stood between life and death.

The foreman stepped towards Steve and grabbed his wrists and squeezed them tight, cutting off the circulation. "I said drop it. There ain't no law out in the forest except our own. And yous know how we treat thieves amongst us...we chop off their hands."

The foreman lifted his axe into the hair and lined the blade up with Steve's wrists. Steve dropped the axe to the ground. He knew the foreman would chop off his wrists if he didn't drop the axe. He didn't want to bleed to death. Living was worth the risk of traveling the woodlands unarmed.

Steve turned and walked away. The crowd around him spread apart. Some of his fellow lumberjacks shouted *coward* as others praised him for this bravery by saying, "You're more a man than I."

The foreman looked about the faces of his men and yelled, "All right now, all ya'll men get back to work, everyone. Ya'll got trees to fall and haul to the Hudson River and float downstream to the mill before winter hits next month. Let's move! These hundred-acres ain't clearin' itself!"

"I'm with Steve, Mr. Foreman."

The foreman turned around. He scanned his men. "Who said that?"

"I did." A lumberjack stepped forward with axe raised above his head, signaling it was he who spoke. "And after the last man was found dead a few nights ago some of us men started talking. We decided that if another body was found, we were gonna walk. And now another one of our brothers has turned up dead. I don't know how serious the other men were but I'm with Steve. I'm quittin' too."

The foreman's face flushed with anger. He raised his axe and pointed it at his men. "If yous men leave this site, don't come back. Keep walkin'. I ain't hiring none of yous back."

"So be it," the lumberjack said, tossing his axe to ground. He turned to the men and shouted, "If any of you is smart, then you'd follow Steve and me!"

The lumberjack pushed through the crowd and headed down the mountain. Behind him, axes fell to the ground in dull thuds as men followed behind.

The foreman turned to his remaining crew and said, "Bonuses for all that stay. Coming out of the deserters pay." He pointed at Ed, "You there, help Sam with Glen's body."

The foreman headed down the slope and when he was out of earshot, Sam said to Ed, "Damn him to hell. He's more worried about makin' his damn quota than seeing that we make it through this job alive."

Ed lifted his axe and swung it into the pine. Pieces of bark exploded from the trunk. He looked at Sam and said, "Must be why he's the foreman. Only cares about getting the job done."

Sam lifted his axe and grunted as he chopped it into the pine. He pulled it out of the trunk and said, "Must be why I'd never make a good foreman."

Ed whacked his axe into the pine. "Well if any more bodies turn up, I'm leaving. Pay or no pay, I'm leaving. I don't want my body stuffed into a hollow tree."

"Not me," Sam said, "As sacred as I am, I have plans and I need that money."

"What plans would those be?"

Sam smiled. Excitement filled his voice. "I hear gold is being found out west. I'll be headin' out there after this job is completed. I'll have enough money saved to ride one of them locomotives to the Rockies. Too dangerous to ride a wagon train with all them Redskins lurking about. I hear they're wild bunches, scalping people and what not."

Ed glanced at Glen's body and shivered at the sight. "I'd rather take my chances with them Redskins too!"

Glen's body was jammed tight inside the tree. His arms were pushed into his body. Broken ribs protruded from his chest. His back was twisted and bent, allowing for his body to be folded with his knees resting on his chest and feet above his head. His body was riddled with different shaped and sized splinters. Dried blood trailed from each point the splinters gouged under his skin. Around his neck was a tree root, wrapped tight enough that the root was partially hidden under the skin.

"TIMBER!" Ed's call echoed across the forest. Three-quarters of the pine crashed to the ground, leaving the section where Glens' body was stuffed still standing.

Sam dropped his axe to the ground and looked down into the trunk at Glen. He bent down and curled his fingers around one of the handles of a two-person saw and lifted. "Grab the other end, Ed. I'm not touching Glen the way he is. We'll have to saw him free."

Ed grabbed the opposite end of the saw. He said, "This makes the eighth body we found in as many weeks."

Sam pushed on the saw. Ed's arms didn't budge on the opposite end. Steve asked, "What's the matter? Come on, get sawin'!"

Ed looked down at Glen's body again and asked, "You don't suppose?"

"Suppose what?"

Ed gulped and leaned over the saw towards Sam and whispered, "A Woodwose?"

Sam laughed. "The Woodwose is just a tall tale. Nothin' more than a story to keep the children from wanderin' the forest alone."

Ed shrugged. "Maybe. Maybe not. It's said though, that when harm is done unto the forest, the Woodwose comes to protect it. When it catches the ones harmin' the forest, the Woodwose entombs its victims inside the hollow of a dead tree. Then the tree feeds off the dead and sprouts new and healthy limbs and leaves."

Sam sighed. "Look, I'm just as nervous as you are but if you keep stallin', sure enough that a Woodwose might just come and get us!"

Ed quickly pushed on the saw. Steve pulled on the opposite end and looked down at the saw blade, guiding it around Glen's body and being careful not to cut into him. Between rakes of the saw upon the trunk, Sam glanced up at Ed and said, "I'm not worried too much about the Woodwose. Besides, I've got other things to worry about. Like how I'm gonna protect all that gold I'll be-a-hulin' out of the mines."

Ed pulled back on the saw at the moment Sam pulled, creating a resistance and grabbing Sam's attention. "Then how do you explain this?" Ed said, pointing at Glen's body. "And how do you explain that every dead lumberjack we found has been jammed inside the hollow of a tree?"

Sam looked down into the tree trunk and then at Ed. "I'm not sure. Let's just free Glen and bury him. We'll worry about some kid's story later."

Ed grabbed the handle and shook his head. "I don't like this at all."

"I don't' either but you just have to stop yer worryin'," Sam said, pulling on the saw. It cut through the trunk lengthwise. Midway through the trunk, Sam stopped sawing and pulled on the bark. The wood crackled and broke free. Glen's body unfolded and flopped out from the trunk and slumped onto the ground.

Ed pushed the saw to the side and kicked away the torn off bark. He said, "Let's hurry up and bury Glen. I'm startin' to think I should get outta here myself."

Sam bent down and hooked his hands under Glen's shoulders. "Where should we bury him?"

Ed shrugged his shoulders. "Don't care, let's just get him buried."

Sam pointed up the mountain. "How about over there behind that boulder? We can etch his name in the rock."

Ed nodded. "Yea, wherever. As long as we do it fast so I can hightail off this mountain."

Sam hooked the fold of his arms under Glen's armpits and Ed grabbed the ankles. Together they lifted Glen's body and carried him up the slope to the boulder and set him on the ground. Sam jabbed a shovel into the soil and stepped down on the spade, driving it deeper into the ground. He pushed down on the handle and tore up the earth. He then lifted up a shovelful of dirt and tossed it over his shoulder. Fifteen minutes into the dig, Steve's arms tired and Ed took over the digging duties. Before his first shovelful, screams echoed up the mountainside from the forest floor below. The screams were high-pitched and filled with pain followed by the tell-tall sound of crackling wood and the distinctive crash of a tree trunk slamming into the ground.

"Oh, Lord!" Sam said, looking over the boulder and down to the mountain base. He looked at Ed and said, "Poor fellow. Got crush by a felled tree."

Ed shook his head in disbelief, removed his Slouch hat and placed it over his heart. "Yea, poor soul." Ed dug into the ground and paused. "Wait...you don't think?"

Sam's facial expression turned from grief-stricken to confusion. He asked, "Think what?"

"That tree, it fell at the base of the mountain."

Still confused, Sam scratched his temple. "What are you gettin' at, Ed?"

Ed pointed down the mountain and then to his left. "We're not clearin' timber down there. Our clearin' area is mapped midway up the slope and to the east."

Sam slowly nodded and looked back down the mountain. "Yup, to the east."

Ed swallowed a lump that clogged up his throat. "Well those screams came from the direction where them quitters went walkin' off to."

"I didn't hear anyone yell *timber*, this mountain carries voices well. Anyone would've heard that call," Sam said, tilting his ear towards the direction the screams came from, hoping to hear chopping or sawing to ease his mind.

Ed whispered, "The Woodwose!"

Both men looked down the mountain and saw the treetops begin to sway and crash into the ground. The treetops then swooped up and straightened before again slamming into the earth. The screams of men at the bottom of the mountain silenced all axes and saws across the forest.

At the bottom of the slope, men sprinted out from the brush, stumbling and lumbering from wounds.

Sam yelled, "Grab your axes! We've got to help them!"

Sam looked behind him. Ed was still standing next to Glen's body. Ed couldn't move; he was frozen by fright.

Sam waved his arm over his shoulder and yelled, "Come on, Ed, they need our help!"

Ed looked down at his axe and reached for it and paused. His eyes widened. The ground under his axe began to undulate as if hundreds of worms were crawling underneath the soil. He bent over and squinted when without warning; roots erupted through the ground, wrapped around Ed's body like a snake and started dragging him underground.

"Ed!" Sam yelled stopping, turning and running back up the slope.

Ed cried out for help as he struggled to free himself from the constricting roots tightening around his torso. The rough surface of the roots scraped across his body, ripping away his clothes and skinning away his flesh. In defense, he dug his fingernails into the fibrous tissue of the roots trying to pry the roots loose from his body.

Unaffected, the roots tightened, causing Ed's lungs to empty and create the feeling of suffocation. His eyes bulged, his teeth grinded and his chest muscles began to spasm. Across his body, he felt all of his muscles tense and start to burn from lack of oxygen.

Sam raised his axe over his head and chopped into the trailing ends of the roots coiled around Ed. With each root that was severed a new root broke through the ground and wrapped around a section of Ed's body. Chop after chop, Sam bore the axe down frantically trying to free Ed until Sam too felt the ground around him soften as roots broke through the ground. They wrapped around his ankles and slithered up his legs.

Sam chopped at the roots twisting around his body. Once freed from their grasps, he scurried up onto the boulder and looked down at Ed. The spot where he was lying as bare expect for hacked up pieces of root and churned soil. Ed was gone. He was pulled underground by the roots.

Screams echoing up the mountain from the foot of the mountain caught Sam's attention. He leapt off the boulder and ran down the slope with axe in hand. Without fearing for his own wellbeing, he ignored the fact that he almost killed himself a short time ago when he had been running down the mountain after finding Glen's body.

He watched as roots twisted around men and squeezed their lives away. He could hear the shattering of their bones. He could see their bodies go limp as they died. He watched as their bodies were pulled apart and strewn across the land.

Not knowing how to defend themselves, men ganged up and chopped at any tree within axe's reach. The landscape turned into a horrific chorus of terror-filled screams and the rustling of leaves and snapping of limbs as trees pummeled the men scurrying across the forest floor.

Sam could see the foreman. He was wielding his axe and burying it deep into the trunk of a pine tree that was whipping its limbs into men as they ran by. With each chop, the pine buckled and swiped its limbs at the foreman's axe until it was swatted away. The foreman turned to run after his axe but was stopped dead in his tracks. A branch crashed down and cracked through his skull, straight through his torso and poked out from his pelvic area. The pine began swinging its branches, impaling lumberjacks within reach.

Sam ran toward the pine and began chopping. Unaffected, the pine continued impaling lumberjacks as it crept its roots towards Sam from behind and wrapped around his neck and torso. The roots lifted him. His legs kicked as he hung five feet off the ground. He dropped his axe and tried pulling the roots off from around his neck.

The roots suffocated him like a python. He felt his ribcage begin to compress. His windpipe was squeezed shut. His eyes rolled into the back of his head and his vision turned black. He could hear multiple axes chopping into the pine's trunk below his feet. But soon, the thump of chopping diminished as his hearing began to lessen.

Sam heard a faint holler of "timber" followed by the crackling of wood as the pine began to fall. His body slammed and bounced off the ground. The roots loosened and Sam was able to uncoil the roots from around his neck and chest. He opened his mouth wide and inhaled deep. He rolled over onto his stomach and began coughing as air filled his empty lungs. His eyesight slowly returned and from the corner of his eyes, he saw the sun glisten off his axe blade.

Sam rolled over and sat up. He stood and ran over to his axe. He reached down to grab it when the dirt around it turned soft. The axe sunk into the soil. Sam fell to his knees and pushed his arm into the ground, feeling blindly for the axe handle. His arm became buried elbow-deep into the ground when he felt a tremor vibrate through his knees. The feeling intensified as it traveled up his legs. His hips began to wobble and his eyes shook, causing his vision to blur. He stood and stumbled forward trying to maintain his balance. As he kept his balance, a mound of earth burbled up under his feet, causing him to lose his footing and tumble and come to rest at the trunk of a weeping willow. He reached up and grabbed the vines and pulled himself up onto his feet.

The vines hanging around him began swaying. The soil around the tree trunk began rippling like water after a pebble breaks the surface. Under Sam's feet the soil churned. The vines wrapped around his wrists and in defense and he pulled on them, snapping them and freeing himself. He backed away and lifted his feet from the burbling earth. Around him, the soil exploded, rocketing clumps of dirt into the air as roots arched and erupted through the topsoil. The roots pushed up from the ground and straightened like octopuses crawling along an ocean floor.

Sam turned and ran away screaming for help but his pleas fell on deaf ears. Ed was dragged underground. The foreman was impaled by a pine tree. Members of the lumberjacking crew were missing, dead, or miles away fleeing for their lives.

Even the lumberjacks who cut down the pine that had hung Sam were gone, dragged away by roots. Large divots pocked the ground with lines trailing into the divots as the men tried digging and clawing their ways out from the holes before disappearing.

Sam turned and ran. Around him, the ground looked as though the earth was reversing itself. The soil churned, exposing tree roots, rolling rocks to the surface and pushing mounds of clay which formed growing mounds of earth that Sam climbed over and rolled down. He jumped to his feet and continued running. The upheaval of earth encased him in clouds of dirt, blinding him from his path. Rocks pelted his body. Twigs punctured and stuck under his skin. Leaves sliced his face open, causing blood to seep down his face and allow his salty sweat to sting his face.

Branches whipped down, creating a swishing sound as they cut through the air. At the last second, blurs of the branches emerged within the dust. Sam ducked, avoiding decapitation. He hunched over and wrapped his arms around his head to shield it from the swooping branches.

As he ran through the clouds of dirt, grains of sand wedged under his eyelids and scratched his eyes. Tears formed and drizzled down his face leaving a trial of mud on his cheeks. His blurred vision made it difficult to navigate within the uproar of trees.

Undaunted, Sam kept running until he felt his feet moistened and the sounds of water splash around his body. He stopped dead in his tracks and looked down. He was standing in a stream. He bent down and dunked his head underwater, opened his eyes and swished his head about and cleaned the dirt from his eyes. After, he raised his head from the stream and wiped his face dry on his shirt.

He looked around the forest. All was quiet and calm. The treetops were still. The roots had retreated underground.

Sam dropped to his knees and knelt in the stream. His chest heaved and he hacked up clumps from dirt from his lungs. Under the sound of his coughing, he felt and heard the familiar rumbling and shockwaves of roots tearing through the ground.

Sam's head turned. The brush behind him started shaking as tree roots emerged from under the bushes and undulated across the ground, pulling their trees behind them like inching caterpillars.

Sam stood to run; but in every direction he turned, roots crept towards him with their trees lumbering behind. Tree branches bent down and dug into the earth, creating a thicket of intertwined branches and leaves, jailing Sam within.

The crackling of wood was deafening as it formed the thicket. Sam dropped to his knees and covered his ears with his hands. His eyes shut tight and he gritted his teeth and fought off the pain within his skull caused by the loud crumbling brush. When all was quiet again, he opened his eyes. Limping towards him; was a hairy and naked man dragging behind his feet, a large and roughly carved club.

The man was bone-thin and stood less than five foot tall. He raised the club over his head and held it like an axe about to split wood. The hairs on his underarms were dreaded and hung like tassels on the ends of drapes. His elbows were bare and calloused over. The hair became thicker on the forearms and thinned out again at the wrists. His hands were also bare. His fingers were caked with dirt and his fingernails were chipped. The skin around his flat and wide nose, black eyes and forehead were also devoid of hair. A nappy beard grew from his cheeks and hung past his neck. The hair growing from his scalp draped over his shoulders and midway down his back. His chest was matted down like short rug shag. The hair thinned at his torso, creating the outline of his hips and thickened again at the thighs. The hair again thinned at his ankles exposing his blackened toenails.

Sam said, "No...no, you're not real. The Woodwose is just a tall tale! This is all nightmare!"

The Woodwose pressed the end of his club into the ground and leaned his elbow in it and looked down at Sam. The Woodwose titled his head like a confused dog. The hairy humanoid acted surprised that his existence was in question.

"Leave me alone!" Sam shouted as he dug his heels into the ground, shuffling his body on his backside, putting distance between himself and the Woodwose.

Sam rolled over and pushed up on his hands and ran towards the thicket. He jumped up and grabbed the tangled branches and roots and began climbing.

The Woodwose tapped his club on the ground three times, summoning a root that broke through the ground. It slithered up the ticket, wrapped around Sam's waist and tugged on his body. Sam's grip on the ticket tightened. He held on for dear life hoping his resistance would snap the root in half and allow him to escape. The root reared back and gave a sharp tug on Sam's body. His grip on the ticket broke. The root then arched and slammed Sam to the ground.

Sam's back arched. He reached behind and pressed the backside of his hand against his back as he breathed through his teeth to ease the pain. Through teary eyes, he saw the Sun become eclipsed by the Woodwose's head and shoulders.

The Woodwose straddled over Sam's body with his club raised. Sam flailed his arms and kicked his legs as he tried knocking the Woodwose off balance. Roots quickly slithered across the ground and wrapped around Sam's ankles and wrists. They tightened and pulled and strapped his legs and arms to the ground.

The Woodwose grunted as he swung the club and bashed it into Sam's temple. The club head tore through Sam's skin, splattering his blood across the ground. The Woodwose continued pounding the club about Sam's body. With each strike, splinters broke off the club and implanted under Sam's skin.

Sam's head flailed back and forth as he screamed and pleaded for his life. Minutes later the only sound heard were the Woodwose's grunts with each swing of the club. Sam's body stopped flinching with each club strike.

He was dead.

The Woodwose was tired and so he stepped away from his victim. He pounded his club upon the ground three times. The roots responded by dragging Sam underground through the soil toward a dead tree where he was pulled up inside the hollowed trunk.

The Woodwose's ears perked up and his head turned toward the mountainside. He frowned and grunted. Echoing over the opposite side of the mountain, a lumberjack's warning yell of "timber" carried over the landscape. The Woodwose pounded his club into the ground, signaling the thicket to separate. The roots and branches untwined, allowing the Woodwose to limp up the mountain toward the lumberjack.

ABOUT THE AUTHOR

Adam P. Lewis emerged on the horror-writing scene in early 2009. His work has appeared in anthologies and in print and digital magazines, all of which have shocked and entertained his readers. Along with fiction, Adam has written articles on writing, book and movie reviews, essays on true crime, and lyrics recorded by nationally and world-wide touring musicians. For more information, please visit http://www.adamplewis.com.

THERE GOES THE NEIGHBORHOOD
(Holiday Version/Extended Cutting)

Brady Allen

"IT'S ALL BULLSHIT," ROBBIE GULMAN SAID. HE STARED AT THE MAW OF THE SMALL underground cave with his friends, all of them positioned around him in a horseshoe shape as he leaned in close. Their bicycles were strewn about behind them in a second horseshoe, creating something of a small amphitheater, like a kids' courtroom within the woods.

The hole was no bigger around than a full-sized pickup tire, but it *was* creepy how the broken rocks had formed something of a crooked-tooth mouth around the entrance. Still—

Danny Gomez put his hands on his hips. He always did this when an argument started, like it emphasized his point more or something. "No, it's not. They *are* down there. It's colder down there, and that's why they stay in there."

"Why do they need it colder? This is all *bullshit*," Robbie said. Saying "bullshit" was Robbie's best tool in an argument. Turning something to bullshit immediately made it false. His nose was dripping watery snot in the chill air, and he pulled up the blue bandana he wore around his neck to wipe it. He was never without a bandana or his cowboy boots.

"Because, you moron," Danny said, his curly black hair springing from beneath his Indians ball cap every which way, "they're from the North Pole. They *have* to have cold. That's why they only sneak out in wintertime."

"If they're from the North Pole, why would they live in Ohio now?"

"They were banished here."

Robbie wasn't exactly sure what banished meant, but it didn't sound good. It sounded a lot like *punished*. "Banished, uh—?"

"By Santa, you moron. He kicked them out."

Okay, now Robbie got it. "Why would Santa banish elves to *Ohio*?"

"Can you think of any worse place?" Danny said.

Robbie shrugged—he liked Ohio—and dug his boot heel into the hard dirt around the cave.

"And they're not elves. They're more like dwarves and...kind of like them, but not really—just dwarves, just hairy dwarf-beasts! But they're like people, kind of."

"Some dwarves *are* people—or people are dwarves," Robbie said.

"They have elf or Santa hats stitched to their heads with this imremov—this unremova—this can't-take-outable thread. Santa punished them for being disloyal. So these hats are permanently sewn into their scalps. And they're made of this…in-des-tructible fabric—can't cut it or anything." He nearly grinned. "Santa is freakin' hardcore."

"How were they disloyal?" Robbie asked.

"Nobody really knows. There are rumors. Groped Mrs. Claus? Maybe molested some reindeer. Bullied and tortured, killed, some toy-making elves…"

None of the other five boys had spoken up yet; they usually let Robbie and Danny go at it for a bit first. Part of it was because Danny seemed so much older than them, seemed to know so much adult stuff.

Now, Conner Billups, the requisite super-chubby friend, said, "*And* they have these enormous claws, Robbie, like big, hooked knives. They can just pop them in and out."

"Retractable," Robbie said. "Bull…*shit!*"

"And they're fast," said Ferd Hinkle, the tallest, skinniest, and slowest of the kids. He looked nervous about this, their speed. "They can move as fast as we blink. I mean, that's how Santa can take presents to every house in one night, right? All things at the North Pole are like that. Super speed!"

"It's all bullshit," Robbie said again. "Even Santa is bull*shit*." And saying this made him feel bigger, a man among nine-year-olds, but he wasn't sure about the Santa thing, really. He *was* getting a little weirded out now, though, looking between the dark rock-teeth and into the throat of the mysterious cave.

"They only take a couple people each year, somewhere near Christmas time," Danny said. "So nobody gets suspicious."

"What do they do when they take people?" Ferd Hinkle said. Robbie could tell Ferd was getting nervous. He'd been tugging at his crotch since he mentioned the super speed. He always tugged on his wiener when he got nervous.

"They *gut* them," Danny said. "Slice 'em up." He made a swiping gesture with his hand, fingers in a crooked claw.

Evening was starting to fall hard now, a late fall evening the Friday after Thanksgiving, and shadows thrown from the trees were starting to close in a, a line of darkness creeping toward the boys' assemblage around the small cave opening.

Robbie unconsciously took a couple steps back from the hole, and Danny moved, too, keeping even with him.

Ferd wasn't staying around any longer, apparently, as he was the first to pick up his bike and swing his leg over it to get ready for the two-mile ride back to their homes over in the suburbs. The cave was in a wooded area owned by the Rivershire MetroParks, and they'd have to ride out of the woods and then through a construction area where yet another new subdivision was being developed outside theirs, the oldest of them all. There were some great dirt hills for ramping where they were digging, but Robbie suspected by the clenched look on Ferd's face that he was going to take the straight and narrow route and get safely inside his house.

The other boys, Connor and Jimmy Grubb and Amos Usserman, took Ferd's lead, climbing on their bikes and getting ready to set out. Robbie hung back with Danny Gomez, though. Despite the fact that he still thought it was all pretty much, well, bullshit, he had a couple of questions, and Danny, whether Robbie liked it or not (with Danny being his debate nemesis and all), seemed to be in the know on this Santa's evil dwarf-beasts matter. Jesus, if that didn't sound silly. But, still—

Danny nodded at Robbie, seeming to know they had a little more debate left in them, a little more business of some sort to attend to, and they told the others to go on ahead, waving to them as they took off, having told them they were going to hang out a little longer and take a different way home.

When they saw chubby Conner Billups puffing away and then leaving their line of sight as he brought up the rear, Robbie said, "Couple questions, Danny."

"Shoot."

"Just pretending this is all true, you know, what do you mean they take a couple people a year near Christmas, these . . . things?"

"If they just attacked the whole neighborhood, well, that'd raise a lot of suspicion, right? They'd be—it's just that people, the police, would go looking—"

"No, I get that," Robbie said. "What I mean is, our neighborhood doesn't lose a couple people each year."

"Yes, it does. It's a big place. It's really all the old suburbs and new subdivisions hooked together."

Robbie hated to admit that Danny usually knew what he was talking about. He was a thinker. He looked into things like adults did. Facts, and all that.

Danny took off his Indians cap and scratched his head thoughtfully, and then he put in back on and said, "Last year. Early December. Olivia Danvers' dad just up and left her and her mom."

Robbie knew there was more to come and waited patiently, even though he really felt that "Robbie versus Danny" urge to debate.

"Well," Danny said, "Olivia's mom had a lawyer search and search and search, so she could get some child support, and *nada...*nothing. Nobody knows where he went."

Robbie shrugged, implying, *That's one.*

"This old guy, you may not know him, Mr. Huerston, he lived out in the back of the neighborhood, on Thurgood Street, where the grass never grew right—?"

"I heard of him," Robbie said. "He's the one who had an accident with his table saw in the garage." Robbie picked up his bike and straddled it.

Danny held up his hand in a stopping gesture. "No accident," he said. "The neighbors heard the screaming, so Santa's Banished Helpers had to get out before they were ready. They probably had to kill him so he wouldn't talk."

"Okay, this is all bullshit," Robbie said. He stood up tall and made to push down on the pedal of his bike. "Santa's Banished Helpers?"

"Wait," Danny said. "Please. I know you think everything I ever say is shit, but . . ."

There was something natural and pained and...*honest* in Danny's voice that made Robbie settle back onto his bike seat and wait. "Go ahead," he said.

"It's true," Danny said. "I've thought about this a lot."

Robbie turned his palms up in a go-ahead gesture.

"Year before. Anita Ramsey, that teenager who ran away? That was a guess that she did because her stepdad was an ass. There was no note or anything. Also, there was this woman who bought a house and never moved in with her son, a third-grader. They just never moved in. Papers had been signed and everything."

Robbie hadn't heard of either of these, but he was listening.

"Year before that, there was Mr. Jensen. Remember? Drowned in the river but his body was never found? And," Danny said, "there was my uncle."

Robbie nodded. All the kids knew to not talk about Danny's Uncle Bennie or you risked Danny going berserk on you. Danny had adored his uncle, who had been living with Danny and his mom and dad. He'd gone missing on the other side of the woods. The side opposite the cave and closer to the construction and the neighborhood. Most people said his uncle had probably just hit the road and was back to being the drifter he'd been before he came to stay with the Gomez family, but Danny and his folks didn't believe it. They'd kept searching the woods well after the local police had stopped doing so.

"It's okay," Danny said. "I know what you want to ask. You're wondering if I think Santa's Banished Helpers got my uncle."

Robbie nodded slightly.

"I know they did," Danny said. "I just know it."

"Why? Why do they take people? Or, uh, gut them?"

"I don't know. But does it matter? It's enough that they do."

Robbie toed the spokes of his front wheel with his cowboy boot. "I'm sorry about your uncle," he said. "He was a cool guy." He *had* been, too—he'd played football with the boys out in the grass a lot, a gentle giant of a man at well over two-hundred pounds. Easy smile and free laugh. Told some good don't-tell-your-parents-who-told-you-this-one jokes, always with a wink.

"Thanks. He was." Danny moved toward his own bike and then unzipped his backpack there, reaching inside. "You wanna help me do something real quick before we go?"

"What?"

Danny pulled several things from his bag: a small gas can, a couple lighters, some ripped-up rags...He looked at Robbie with a determined set of his face. "Smoke those freakin' things down in the cave?"

Robbie didn't say anything.

"For my Uncle Bennie," Danny said.

And, of course, Robbie had to say okay.

Kendall Knapp opened the white picket gate at the back of his yard and dragged his trashcans from the side of his garage to the alley behind it. He hated his white picket fence with a passion—it'd been one of the only things he didn't like about the house when he'd bought it almost two years ago—but he just didn't have the time or money to replace it with chain link or something else right now. Maybe when summer came around.

Today, just two days after Thanksgiving, was pretty nice: a gray-skied Ohio Saturday, low forties at 1 p.m. and no wind. Up and down his street and alley all day, he'd seen many of his neighbors dragging Christmas decorations from their garages to their houses, seen them leaving empty-armed in their cars, only to return with bags from Target and Walmart and stores from the mall. The preternatural Perrys had green and red tinsel woven through their own white picket fence, and the always overzealous Roger Gebhart was on his extension ladder looping Christmas lights around the branches of his front-yard blue spruce tree.

Besides his hunter green trash cans, the most festive thing Kendall had going in his yard at this point were the brown and brittle chrysanthemums along one fencerow in his back yard waiting to have a go at it again next spring. Maybe he should at least hang a wreath on his door. Or go all out and get one of those big inflatable snowmen for his front yard.

The Heiden kid, Michael, was shooting hoops on the portable basket in the alley two doors down. He waved when he saw Kendall and said, "Hey, Mr. Knapp! We won our JV game last Tuesday!"

"Great!" Kendall said. "How'd you do, Michael?"

He was a polite kid. Kendall liked him. And tall. Maybe 6'2" at 14 or 15. Couple inches more and he's pass Kendall. He had his hair shaved close to his skull and was always outside shooting hoops with a hooded sweatshirt pulled up on his head, no matter how warm or cold it was.

"I scored 16 points! I've been working on a new post move. Want me to show you?" Michael asked.

"Sure, let me drag my last few trash cans around and then I'll come over."

"Cool." And then the ball was pounding the alley pavement again.

Trash day was Monday, but Kendall always forgot to drag his cans around if he waited until Sunday evening. He viewed himself as irresponsible, but responsible enough to recognize this—he liked to keep one step ahead of his irresponsibility.

When he was pulling the last overloaded can around to the back of the garage, he was greeted by Jackson Beard, drunk as he often was, going on and on about Christmas shopping and these "asshole consumers not needing this garbage" and "the whole neighborhood going to crap because of the damn capitalism and false advertising." He waved to old Mr. Beard and said, "I'm getting rid of *my* garbage, sir" and actually got a smile and a wave out of the old guy.

After Mr. Beard had moved along and turned the alley corner, Kendall closed his gate and heard the familiar sound of the basketball clanging off the side of the rim. Michael liked to shoot from way out but didn't have that range. Kendall was sure he got most of his points scrapping under the boards and pulling down offensive rebounds.

He turned to look for the ball rolling his way, and there were three images right in a row that would stick with Kendall for the remainder of his life: first, the orange Rawlings basketball rolling down the alley toward him; second, Michael Heiden's head lying in a blooming puddle of blood several feet from his body, straight out from the hoop; and third, the malformed beast with the razor claws and singed fur and charred Santa Claus hat suddenly in front of him slicing open his stomach and splattering his blood all over his white picket fence.

One minute and forty seconds: that's how long these images were part of his breathing life and how long it took his guts to fall out in a heaping pile in the alley.

Jessica McManus saw the start of it from her attic bedroom window, her hair up in a towel and another wrapped around her torso, less than a minute after exiting the steamy upstairs bathroom in her parents' house. She used to babysit Michael Heiden when he was six or seven and she'd been fourteen. Now here she was nearing college graduation and he was a high school basketball player who'd been well over six-foot tall before his head had been sliced clean from his body by some kind of scissor-handed simian Santa.

She didn't scream. The desire to do so had been there, and she opened her mouth for one, but all that had come out was a low, dumb humming sound: *Nunh-nnnnnnnh-nunh-nnnnnnnh*, which she soon realized was the beginning of the word she wanted to say: *No*. And soon enough, she said it, rather meekly at first: "No." And then she couldn't stop saying it: "No no no no nononono no . . ."

She unconsciously readjusted the towel tucked tightly together at her armpit. She felt exposed there in the window, but she couldn't bring herself to move, to stop looking, and she remembered Michael Heiden as a kid then, so clearly, how he'd had a little-boy crush on her and had even started to call her Jess-Mommy after she'd been babysitting for a year and then his parents had a gotten a divorce, his mom so busy with her career that she'd actually settled for the shaft no-custody visitation that so many dads got. How he'd always wanted to cuddle with her when they watched cartoons together or how he liked that she rubbed his hair and scalp with her fingernails to get him to go to sleep.

And now she stared down into the alley at his head and a face barely even old enough to shave and pictured his body rising from the asphalt and gravel and picking up the head and slipping it back on his torso like a Halloween mask. But, of course, it didn't. Michael didn't rise up and wave to her, reassembled, with an ornery smile.

And then there was Mr. Knapp—a huge man (everyone called him if they needed something heavy moved)—standing there stunned, looking at Michael and absurdly trying to collect his own entrails that were spilling out of him like a haphazardly placed fire hose slipping from its truck. Jessica was momentarily amazed at just how much could fall out of a person in terms of internal organs, and then she vomited her tuna sandwich and sweet pickles against the window pane. And just as seeing your own puke will make you want to puke, she brought the last of her lunch up into her mouth and spit it onto the hardwood floor where it splattered and made her want to lose her groceries a third time—if there'd been any left.

Jessica whipped the towel from her head and wiped her mouth and chin on it and then tossed it in the corner of the room.

Outside the window, Mr. Knapp finally fell face-first into his intestines and stopped moving.

"No no no no no nononono no!" She realized that she was shouting now, and she jerked her body (or it did so on its own), and the towel fell from her torso, just as she heard a scream from downstairs. Her mom? She must've gotten home from shopping while Jessica was in the shower. Her mother had no problem screaming, it seemed, and now Jessica *could* move her feet. She reached down and grabbed the clean towel from the floor and ran out of the room and to the staircase, trying all the while to put the towel back in place.

She made it halfway down the wooden stairs and then her foot landed awkwardly, the back of her heel just catching a stair and then slipping to the next. She landed on her ass, the towel a non-issue left behind now, righted herself, hit the last few stairs squarely, and then turned the corner toward the living room and the front entryway. A chill breeze hit her naked skin, her nipples woke up (God, what a time for *that*!), and she turned the corner to find the front door wide open.

And to see her mother, her long fall coat hanging half off, dragged through the door lickity split, her fingers digging for purchase futilely, a thin smear of blood left behind.

Jessica stood stunned for a few seconds, which may have, she thought later, saved her own life. Leaving, of course, the guilt about whether or not she could have saved her mother. Though as she would see more and more what was happening, she'd decide that she definitely could *not* have. Still, guilt would hang on like a bur.

When she could finally move again, she bolted to the front door, stepping to the side of her mother's blood, and looked out. There was no sign of her mom—whatever had taken her (one of those ape-things?) had done it fast. Jessica whipped the front door shut, threw the deadbolt, and then, naked as the day she'd exited her mother's womb, went for the kitchen phone.

If Robbie Gulman hadn't just finished taking a leak, he'd have pissed himself. He was waiting for Danny Gomez to get there, as planned, so they could ride to the school football field and play until someone kicked them off, and he'd just finished peeing outside beneath the big apple tree in the back of his parents' yard (he liked how the cool air gave him full bladder contraction—he could piss a mile!), when he heard the scream.

This weird feeling came over him that this had something to do with he and Danny shoving piles and piles of kindling into the cave (branches and leaves, mostly) the evening before and then lighting and dropping those gas-soaked torches to follow. He just *knew* it. Like he knew his mom was going to fall off the stepping stool one time when she was cleaning a ceiling light fixture. He knew it before she even got on the stool.

The cave.

The scream: it came from two doors down—Ferd Hinkle's house. It was Ferd's mom. The piercing scream, and then, "Help! My gawwwwd! Something's in the house! Something killed my boy! *Heeeelp!*" Robbie looked across the fencerows and saw Mrs. Hinkle standing in their backyard with an apron on, waving her arms frantically.

The scream in and of itself was not piss-worthy, but what happened next was:

Mrs. Hinkle, amid her arm-waving and yelling caught sight of Robbie. "My gawwwwd!" she screamed again. "Robbie! Robbie! Get your dad! Get your—"

Someone or some*thing* burst through the Hinkles' backdoor.

Mrs. Hinkle turned toward it, her scream cutting off nice and neat as you please, and then—and this is where Robbie's bladder contracted again, but there was nothing left to come out—this small hairy man, this *thing*, was on Mrs. Hinkle in less than a snap of the finger, and in a matter of seconds (and then a few), Ferd's mom was scattered about their backyard, a hand here, her scalp there, the contents of her stomach splattered across one of her bird feeders.

This thing, it turned toward Robbie then, and it smiled. He noticed for the first time some sort of ragged red hat pulled tightly over its skull. It had overly large teeth, and despite all of its fur, its tangled hair, Robbie thought there was something still very human in the way it moved. *A dwarf-beast?* When it raised its arm in a curling-claw wave, razor talons sinister for their extreme length, well, that's when Robbie ran for the house to find his dad.

He ran as hard as he could but felt he was moving too slowly. When he reached the backdoor and had his hand on the handle, he risked a look back, expecting that smiling dwarf-beast to pounce. But there was no sign of it, the thing, what Danny Gomez would surely have called a Santa's Banished Helper.

Ferd. Dead. Robbie explicably wondered if he'd died nervously tugging on his wiener or if he had put up a fight. And then he felt ridiculous and sad for having thought so.

Robbie stepped inside, the back door leading to a room they used as a recreation room (TV, toys, beanbag chairs, a desk and computer). He didn't call out; he was afraid to make noise. He walked slowly through the room and into the kitchen next. The heels of his cowboy boots seemed to *clock-clock* too loud.

His mom was out Christmas shopping, and when he'd gone out back to pee and wait for Danny, his dad had been in the living room up front, watching TV. He could hear the TV now and breathed just a little easier, picturing his dad on the couch with his feet propped on the coffee table.

He crept through the kitchen to the living room, but his dad was not in there. A basketball game was on the television. He started to move to the staircase, but he heard a sound coming from the fireplace, from up the chimney flue. There was a grunting and a squishing. And there was a lot of blood on the stones.

Robbie Gulman nearly screamed, but he held it. God's will, he held it in. He backed into the kitchen and eyeballed his dad's cell phone on the counter. He grabbed it and grabbed a big knife from the kitchen drawer below it. He punched 911 on the cell phone and headed through the recreation room and toward the back door. But the phone was not charged. Dead.

Mr. Knapp down the alley. Kendall Knapp. That's where he'd go for help. He was a smart guy, a big tough guy. He could help. Dad always had him over to help move big things. Plus, he played chess. Everybody who played chess was smart.

Robbie opened the backdoor and hit the yard running, knowing the more he thought about it, the harder it would be to get moving. He sprinted with the knife held out to the side just like his dad had taught him to hold a knife when walking. Only when he reached the back fence did he allow himself to look behind. At first he didn't see anything, but then he heard noise coming from the roof of the house. Something breaking. He looked up to see bricks sliding down the shingles onto the back porch. The chimney was wrecked. Two of the dwarf-beasts were up there, one of them jumping up and down and almost laughing, an excited growl of sorts. The other was pulling something through what remained of the chimney.

It was an arm.

Robbie now knew for certain where his dad was.

Still, he didn't scream. Robbie reached down somewhere inside himself and found that little sprout of a man that still had a lot of growing to do, and he held fast.

He turned away, tears filling his eyes and spilling onto his cheeks. He tossed the knife over the fence, put the cell phone in his pocket, and climbed over, grabbing the knife after he landed on the other side. Mr. Knapp's was halfway down the alley, thirty seconds at a sprint, maybe. Robbie hoped to God that he was home. And alive.

Kendall Knapp was not alive, however; he was, of course, doing the dead man's face-plant in his own tumbled guts. Nine-year-old Robbie Gulman would discover that soon enough.

All around the neighborhood, there was carnage: Roger Gebhart's extension ladder was still leaned against his blue spruce tree, his Christmas lights half strung, but he was not on it. Not all of him anyhow. A little spatter here, a little smudge there. Here a clump, there a clump. Most of him was laid out at the bottom of the ladder, a corpse in a gruesomely-open but should've-been-closed, suburban, manicured lawn coffin. Car doors were open, bodies hanging out, front doors to houses flung wide, occupants in an array of poses on their front lawns. Santa's Banished Helpers were everywhere: rooftops, running down the streets, jumping around on backyard trampolines, swinging from telephone and power lines. There were sirens and shouts and screams. The Perrys, their white hair stained red, were propped up in their front porch chairs, their heads severed and replaced on each other's body. Animals had been untouched by the Santa's Banished Helpers, and dogs howled and sniffed and growled at their own shadows. Cats carried fingers in their tiny mouths and yowled from trees.

Just how many of these Santa's Banished Helpers there were, it was impossible to tell. These hairy little men, these dwarf-beasts, these simians with claws, growled and grinned and moved with deadly precision and a ghastly sense of festivity. They relished in destruction and evisceration, were enraptured in such deviant frolic. Despite their derisiveness and dark play, they moved with such speed and killed with such ease that there could have been four, there could have been a hundred. It didn't really matter. This town was being painted red.

***

The kitchen phone had not, of course, worked. Jessica had figured as much on some level, but you just had to try it or wonder later. If there was much *later* left for her that was—it sounded alternately like a war and a party outside now.

The first thing she needed to do was get back upstairs and grab something to wear. Fight, flight, it didn't matter, not naked—she'd do it better with some clothes on.

Jessica walked back to the staircase but stopped at the bottom. There were noises coming from upstairs. She put one foot on the bottom stair and tilted her head. There was shuffling up there, grunting. She leaned over farther and the stair squeaked. Now there was growling, a loud crash.

Jessica backed out, turned, and bolted for the back sliding door. It was locked, but she flipped it quickly, slid it open, and ran through the backyard toward the alley, still not a stitch of clothing on and her hair soaking wet. She bounded across the yard and pulled open the free-standing garage entrance, stepped inside, and shut the door behind her.

Enough light came in through the side windows so that Jessica could see pretty well. She very quickly grabbed two things: a rain poncho, which she pulled over her head and wiggled into, and an ax. So she wouldn't be trapped if one of those things came in after her, she hit the garage door opener, but it didn't work.

She was thinking rationally still, though, and the poncho made her feel, well, less naked, less vulnerable, and she went to the door and opened it manually.

As soon as she had it open, she heard footsteps clip-clopping in the alley. Jessica raised the ax and wielded it like a baseball bat. She peeked around the corner of the open garage door in the direction of the (running, clearly) footsteps: it was a kid in cowboy boots and a bandana, holding a big kitchen knife out to the side. She recognized him but didn't *know* him, really. Gulman. He was the Gulman kid.

Jessica gestured for him to come to her. "Come here, come on!"

But the kid skidded to a halt, his eyes on something else in the alley. He dropped his knife and bent over at the waist. He was crying, she could see now. "Aw, man," he said. "This is bullshit. It's all *bullshit!*"

She looked where he was looking. There were none of those simian things that she could see. But there was Mr. Knapp and his pile of innards and Michael Heiden and his head. That must've been what stopped the Gulman kid's sprint down the alley.

"Bullshit!" the kid said again. "Mr. Knapp is dead. Mr. Knapp is *dead!*"

"Hey," Jessica said. "Look here. Gulman, right? What's your first name again?"

No response. The kid was crying harder now. "Bullllllshiiiit!" he screamed.

"Hey!" Jessica screamed now. "Come here!"

The Gulman kid looked her way. She motioned for him again. There were several growls and some animal-like laughter from several directions, and this got him moving. When he reached the garage, she asked again, "What's your first name?"

"Robbie." His crying stopped suddenly and he looked her over, clearly puzzled by the poncho.

"I was in the shower," she explained and felt silly for doing so. "Okay, Robbie. I'm Jessica. I think we need to stick together and find a place to hide."

"Have you seen how fast they are?" he said. "It's just like Ferd—" He cut himself off sharply and looked like he might cry again.

"This is a lot to deal with," Jessica said, "but we have to hide. And *now!*"

Someone was screaming from far down the alley, and it was getting closer fast. In a couple of seconds, Jessica realized whoever was doing so was calling Robbie Gulman's name: *Roooobieeee!*

Robbie heard it, too, because he said, "It's Danny. My friend Danny. We were supposed to meet."

They both leaned out the big garage door opening, and Jessica saw a young curly-haired boy with his ball cap turned backwards pedaling his bike through the alley like a bat out of hell. She and Robbie both signaled for him to stop and turn in at the same time.

"Robbie!" the boy said, and he braked hard and cut his handlebars toward the garage, terror obviously overtaking grace as he crashed into Mr. McManus's leaf blower, causing a domino effect of falling tools and appliances. It didn't slow Danny Gomez, though—he was off his bike like that and turning every which way.

Robbie Gulman grabbed him by the arm, and Danny responded by clenching Robbie's bandana in his fist and saying, "We did this. *I* did this!"

"Listen, boys," Jessica said, "we need to find a place to hide. A place to get our bearings and figure out what we can do."

"Mr. Knapp's basement," Robbie said. "He's got guns and food down there. But these things are too fast for gu—"

"It's a temporary plan," she said. "Let's do it." Jessica had seen all the best zombie movies. These were the two things they needed most: food and guns. They could be holed up for a while.

They left the garage armed to the teeth, at least as much as they could be: Danny with a baseball bat and a keyhole saw, Jessica with the ax, and Robbie with the big kitchen knife and a can of hornet spray.

Mr. Knapp's house was just across the alley and one door down.

Robbie was in the lead, Jessica in the middle, and Danny covering the back. Robbie felt a sense of importance that kept him more alert but feeling *less* alert, at once, seeing as how Jessica had trusted him to lead and was clearly naked beneath that poncho. A college girl. He was no longer nine, he was eighteen.

It was a short walk, but the growling and grunting was everywhere, consistently threatening and directionally indistinguishable. But it was a short walk. That's what Robbie kept telling himself, anyhow. Just across the alley on a slight diagonal, find a door unlocked (they were betting on Mr. Knapp's side door), get in, and get to the basement.

Crossing they alley was when they were most vulnerable, but it was the easiest, too. A quick sprint, a step around Mr. Knapp's body, and they were through his blood-splattered picket gate in five seconds.

Santa's Banished Helpers were on rooftops, hanging from power and phone lines, walking along fence rows. It seemed like there were an impossible number of them, and if you blinked they were somewhere else a considerable distance from where they'd just been.

Robbie didn't want to see one any closer than he had in the Hinkles' yard. They were foul beyond imagination. To see those elongated teeth up close, those claws, and that stitched-on hat, the tufts of fur and burned skin right up close—

We did this. Danny and me.

—well, he didn't think he'd be able to move.

Now, though, he led Jessica and Danny in a sprint through Mr. Knapp's backyard and to the side door. He opened the storm door and tried the wooden one behind it. Locked. Shit.

"Use the knife," Danny said.

Robbie just looked at him. He wasn't sure what he meant.

"Here," Danny said and took the knife and moved Robbie aside. Robbie watched him in awe, as Danny showed that grown-up side once again, chipping away at the doorframe around the lock with the big chopping knife, until there were wood splinters all around his feet...and...the lock popped when Danny turned the knob.

And they were in.

They went straight to the basement, its door and staircase in the direct center of the house, Danny in the lead now, having won this spot somehow with his ability to get the side door open. Robbie brought up the rear, pulling the door closed behind him as they descended the wooden staircase.

It was nearly dark down there, the gray day barely making its way through the glass-block windows high up on three of the four walls. Robbie tried the light switch at the bottom of the stairs. They were all surprised when the ceiling bulbs came on, and not surprised when they went out just as fast. Robbie was left seeing spots for a moment.

There was tons of canned food on aluminum shelves in the old cold storage room. Robbie mentioned quietly that he hoped they could find some flashlights down here and then he showed them the gun cabinet. Mr. Knapp had showed Robbie and his dad his array of guns down here a couple of times. Robbie's dad was something of a gun guy, too. The cabinet was a tall steel structure behind some folding doors. It was secured with a thick, steel, heavy-duty cabinet lock.

"And we don't have the key," Robbie said. He looked at Jessica, and his heart dropped. He'd had the idea to come down here, and now he'd failed them. "I'm so stupid. Mr. Knapp would have the key on the ring in his pocket."

"Do you two even know how to shoot guns?"

"Shot them with my uncle," Danny said. "Yeah."

Robbie thought again about the two of them setting fire in the cave. He honestly hadn't even thought the fire would stay lit very long, that the torches and kindling would all just fall down the cave and scatter and go out.

"Same here. With my dad," Robbie said. "Just .22's," he admitted, though. "Got low recoil."

Jessica shrugged. "Not me," she said. "I've never shot one. Didn't believe in them."

"We need them," Danny said matter-of-factly. "Have you seen these things?"

"Santa's Banished Helpers," Robbie said, and Danny nodded grimly.

"I saw some people putting up a fight, and these freakin' things...would...*not*...go down."

"You think we have to shoot them in the head?" Jessica said. "Like zombies."

"I don't have any better ideas," Danny said. "They're not brainless. This has been a very, uh, coordinated attack. But confident—they've been playing with us."

There goes Danny the Adult again, Robbie thought. But right now he was glad of it.

"You make it sound like a war game," Jessica said. "Well, if that's the case—let's get ready. Robbie, look around for tools that can get that gun cabinet open."

"Mr. Knapp's tools are in his garage," he said.

"He could have a few down here. Check those shelves over there. Danny, look around to see what we could brace the basement door with."

She was the oldest, so Robbie and Danny went with it. When they were both busy, Robbie heard Jessica's footsteps running up the basement stairs. The door opened and then slammed shut. Her footsteps continued through the house and then stopped when she heard the side door slam closed.

Robbie and Danny stared at each other.

Then it dawned on Robbie. "She's going for the keys," he said.

Danny nodded. "I hope she freakin' gets them," he said.

Being cautious with these things, these simian beasts, didn't matter. They were too fast, Jessica understood. And so she took the house, the side door, the backyard, and the alley, all at a dead sprint and made it cleanly to Mr. Knapp and his spilled intestines. What she couldn't do so quickly, however, was convince herself to reach down into the big dead man's pocket.

She replayed Mr. Knapp and Michael Heiden's executions in her mind. Saw again, too, her mother being pulled out the front door in a sudden, wrenching tug. She looked down the alley at Michael's head and torso lying a few feet apart and remembered caressing his scalp to get him to sleep when he was a young boy.

She thought of the two boys down in Mr. Knapp's basement waiting, hoping, she guessed, for her return. Jessica hoped they didn't follow after her.

Squatting down, her poncho crinkling, Jessica rolled Mr. Knapp over, his face coming free from his guts with a wet sucking sound. His key ring was in the first pocket she checked, and she wiggled her hand in there, working the keys free. She had them in her hand when she looked up while starting to stand.

And she saw the strange beast standing there and grinning at her.

Robbie and Danny briefly debated and considered going after Jessica, but their minds were made up for them. Less than thirty seconds after she'd bounded up the stairs on her apparent quest for the gun cabinet keys, there'd been a commotion of grunting and growling upstairs and the sound of at least a couple sets of feet moving around above them.

The boys held their fingers to their lips and shushed each other simultaneously. Robbie held the big kitchen knife and Danny the baseball bat. The other items had been set down somewhere, and Jessica had taken the ax, it seemed.

A very loud sound shook the floor above them, followed by a series of crashes, glass breaking, things rolling across hardwood. And then something was dragged or pushed across the floor and, Robbie realized, pushed against the basement door.

"The refrigerator," Danny whispered. "They've trapped us down here."

Robbie felt like he wanted to scream but held it. "And Jessica up there," he said.

Jessica's fate was to be determined with the beast that leered at her across Mr. Kendall Knapp's devastated body. She was not transfixed, was not frozen in terror, but, rather, she was waiting.

Waiting.

To see what this thing would do.

She absorbed every detail: there was an elf-like hat that appeared to be a permanent part of its head, black char-marks on it, but it was otherwise the cleanest part of the whole creature, red with a white ball hanging from its elongated tip—a Santa hat, really; the beast was hairy, but not really furry, covered in tufts and patches of thick hair, but there were other spots where it seemed the hair had been burned away; it was upright and powerfully built, stunted and dwarflike but obviously agile and strong and quick; it was naked but for the hat, and as she looked along its torso, its hairy drooping penis grew instantly rigid and pointed at her, wagging excitedly.

Jessica looked up quickly, right into its face. And that's when she knew just how dangerous this thing was. There was something entirely human enough in its cold leering eyes to make it seem that much more dangerous.

She dropped the keys, which she held in one hand, and then she swung the ax with two hands, aiming for that turgid, monstrous penis.

And she missed. She was not even close.

This beast was way too fast. She was not at all shocked to see that her poncho had been very precisely sliced in half lengthwise in the front while she swung, and it hung open, exposing her pubis and her breasts.

The beast now had claws like she'd seen on the one that had taken down Michael and Mr. Knapp.

She swung the ax again and again, the beast sidestepping and growling, occasionally taking a lick from the ax—once on the shoulder, once on the leg, but just as soon as the wounds opened up, they started to seal themselves, and Jessica understood that even if she had chopped that grotesque monster dick right off, another would have eventually taken its place. Whatever these things were, the suburbs didn't stand a chance.

Jessica swung the ax until her arms could do it no more.

And then the beast with those cunning human eyes was on her. And in her. And eventually her innards were mixed with Mr. Knapp's and her poncho was nothing more than macabre party streamers twisting down the alley.

So, these two boys, nine years old, one a man almost before he'd been a boy, another trying so hard every day to be one but still so far away, they sat in a cold basement in a dead neighbor's home and ate cold potato slices from a can cut open by a big kitchen knife. They leaned back against an impenetrable gun cabinet that was held fast by a steel lock. They'd been down there for over a week—it was December now according to a digital watch they'd found in a drawer—and they had heard nothing more than occasional footsteps on the floor above them. A couple of times, they'd tried opening the basement door at the top of the stairs, but what they assumed was the refrigerator would not budge.

"Danny?" this one boy said. He was wearing a bandana around his neck and his cowboy boots were crossed at the ankle.

"Yeah?" the other boy, Danny, said. His dark curls were greasy and hanging lifeless beneath his Indians ball cap.

"What do you think they plan to do with us?"

"I'd say with the legends seeming true, they're holding us here. Trying to bait Santa, so they can get some freakin' revenge."

"Bullshit. There's no Santa." But this boy did not believe that was true. Not anymore.

"Man, Robbie. When are you going to—?"

The scanner they'd found here in Mr. Knapp's basement crackled to life. They recognized the voice of Mr. Beard, the former notable town drunk: *We shouldn't have fed it . . . the suburban, commercial (he spoke this as commersssshhhhial) Christmas monster. This...is...all...your fault.*

"There he goes again," the boy named Danny said. "Freakin' drunk."

"Yeah," said Robbie. "This is *our* fault." He felt like crying but didn't, as happened to him a lot, and he thought of their torches being dropped into the rock-toothed maw of the cave in the woods.

"Bullshit," said Danny. And they both got a slight chuckle out of this, despite their shared awareness of things to come, their odds of survival.

Because...

Up the stairs.

Beyond the refrigerator.

Through Kendall Knapp's house.

Out the side door.

It was a different neighborhood.

These dwarves. These simians. These men. These beasts.

They'd decorated for the holidays.

Shriveled ears and hands and penises and organs long past recognition hung from trees and bushes. Intestines were strewn about fences like garland. Green pine and spruce and fir trees were washed with dried blood, once red. Bodies were piled in nativity scenes gone gruesomely awry. Police cars sat abandoned and useless, their sworn occupants strewn about the carnage, faces rotting away with their surprised looks.

No one else came near this place, no one even thought to, the dark magic of these shunned North Pole helpers as perfected as the precise swipes of their claws.

They sat on porches and strolled the sidewalks; they drank and they caroused and they made the neighborhood their own; they laughed and leapt about and made merry and waited for that day not so far away.

When they would hear sleigh bells. And their time would come. As they knew it would.

They old man would make his trip, and their plan would unfold: Children locked into basements with care. In hopes that fat bastard could not leave them there.

ABOUT THE AUTHOR:

Brady Allen grew up in a small country town in southern Ohio and now lives and writes in Dayton, Ohio. He published nearly thirty short stories between 1999 and 2004 in the genres of horror, dark fantasy, crime, and soft sci-fi, among others, but horror is his main squeeze. Some places his work appeared include *Crimewave* in England, *The Black Mountain Review* in Northern Ireland, and in horror anthologies with Delirium Books and Eraserhead Press. Two of his stories, "Slow Mary" and "Six Miles From Earth," were selected as honorable mentions in St. Martin's Press's *Year's Best Fantasy and Horror* anthologies, and he is a past recipient of an Individual Fellowship in Fiction from the Ohio Arts Council. After a hiatus from writing and publishing fiction, he's back at it and going strong with nearly a dozen short story submissions out there. He's just finishing revisions on a dark fantasy novel called *The Disharmony of Frogs* and is well into the first draft of a draft of a horror novel. Two short story collections are in the works: just completed is *Back Roads and Frontal Lobes*, and the second is still untitled. You can find out more and read free fiction at www.bradyallen.com.

Yellow

John Everson

I**N THE COOL KISS OF A SUN-DRENCHED DAWN, SO MUCH CAN BE DISMISSED, SO MUCH** forgotten.

But it's hard to dismiss the empty space in the bed beside me last night.

It's hard to ignore the brick red stains that mar the otherwise bleached pebbles on the dry streambed down the hill.

And it's impossible to still the voice behind my eyes that screams "yellow, yellow, yellow" without pause or compassion. The voice names me truly. I can brook no argument.

Ostensibly it was solitude for my writing which brought Rachel and me to this backwoods cabin two months ago, but there was an underlying agenda to our relocation as well. We hoped, no, we wondered, if spending time together could pump vigor back into our flagging marriage. I can't say that we both wished that our life together could be saved. Call it wistful curiosity. We treated it more as some kind of psychological experiment in human emotion. Consign the two rats to an otherwise rat-free cage and what will they do? Reproduce, or consume each other. It was a move of joint desperation, not hope.

Perhaps it was that lack of hope that ultimately caused Rachel's doom. If we had acted together, as one, so many things might have been different. But the two rats found a third alternative. They neither mated nor chewed each other. Instead, amid the lazy birdsongs of the forest, we simply retreated to our own corners of the cabin. She withdrew into a correspondence course on computer languages, and I? Well, as many "retreat" writers may admit, did not write. Instead, I spent an increasing amount of time away from the cabin, exploring the miles of hilly wooded trees around us.

The upshot of all this is, when I discovered the cave during one of my daily walks along the dry streambed, I didn't, as many a mate would, run back to drag Rachel out to the spot. I held it to myself jealously.

It seemed like a small cave, when I first pushed the cascade of weedy leaves aside and peered inside. My stomach trembled, as I expected at any moment to hear the growl and meet the unforgiving jaws of a black bear or some similar unfriendly animal. But I could smell no spoor as my head hung just inside the lip of the opening. I ducked and slowly poked my body in, now adding snakes and scorpions to my "to be worried about" list.

"Hello?" I called, and then listened intently for any telltale movements. There were none.

I couldn't see how far the cavern extended to the sides, but I could, from the dim light the cleared entrance allowed in, see that the front cavern of the cave narrowed to a tunnel that continued into the mountainside. It took every bit of restraint I owned to not barrel into that corridor right then. I was a child again, and I had found a secret place to call mine.

"I'll be back tomorrow," I called out loud, and smiled as my voice vaguely echoed in the hidden recesses of the cave.

I don't know what Rachel thought when I got home that evening. I'm sure my face beamed with secret pride at my discovery. She glanced at me oddly a couple times over dinner.

"What is with you tonight?" she asked at one point.

"Just a beautiful day, I guess," was my empty reply.

That night as she lay beside me in bed, I reached out to massage her chest, but she pushed my hand away.

"No," she whispered. A while later as I fumed in unfulfilled lust beside her, I felt the bed shake in a rhythm I recognized. It was not erotic. She was crying.

The cave had once been inhabited by something. Where the front cavern ceiling diminished to meld with the silty floor lay stacks of dried brush. The former bed of bear and 'coon, I thought, and flashlight in hand, I pushed my way deeper into the cave, to begin the exploration of the tunnel beyond that first small cavern. Would it only peter out to an impassable crack in the mountain, or lead to more geological treasure rooms within? I ached to find out.

I had come prepared. My backpack held spare flashlight batteries, a canteen, a hammer and a variety of snacks. After hearing horror stories all my life of unlucky and unprepared spelunkers, I had attached an end of twine to a tree just outside the cave lip. The spool hung from my belt, unwinding a guideline back to daylight with every hesitant step I strode.

As I moved into the murky recesses of the earth, my mind kept returning to Rachel. This should have been a shared excursion, I growled to myself, blaming her for our current lack of connection. Never mind that I hadn't asked her to come with me.

I found a bitter laugh in the memory of the two of us bicycling down the slope of a volcano on Maui so many years before. In the pregnant predawn grey, we'd weaved back and forth on the descending slope, pedaling close enough for me to reach out and hold her hand—a romantic and foolhardy thing to do when whizzing with almost no control down the slope of a mountain. My situation now was so completely opposite. I thought.

The tunnel did not, as I'd feared, taper off to a dead end, but instead, angled slowly upwards. Its sides were nearly smooth, completely unlike the haphazard crash of rock and boulder on the outside of this mountain. They glistened in the yellow light of the flash with wetness. The air seemed humid and strangely warm, not at all the clammy cool of deep earth I'd expected and dressed for. Soon I was tying my jacket around my waist by its arms, and sweat was running freely down my cheeks and neck. And the tunnel continued, slowly but inexorably sloping upwards, towards what pinnacle I could not guess.

I stopped and wolfed down a bag of Doritos, then emptied half the canteen at the thirst they brought. Not, perhaps, the wisest choice in snacks. Still, refreshed and having caught my breath, I continued forward then. How long was this tunnel? Would I simply exit halfway up the mountain and then have to stumble my way home back down the outer face of the rock? Or would the trail end and leave me forced to retrace my seemingly endless steps straight back down? The sense of adventure in exploring an underground labyrinth was giving way to boredom and exhaustion. And the deep blackness which the light of my flash couldn't completely disrupt was giving me a slight case of claustrophobia.

After an hour or more of walking, I was strongly considering giving up and turning around. This was no doubt a sluice tunnel from the spring thaws that simply had burrowed into the outer skin of the mountain and wended its way down to the valley, never branching, never creating any of the stalactite wonder I was hoping to find.

But then I heard the rush of water. It was faint, just a whisper, but unmistakable. My goal was not too far away. I redoubled my steps and the trickle grew in my ears until the tunnel abruptly ended in a cavern 10 times the size of the one at the entrance end of the passage.

The flashlight only barely cut the gloom to trace out the slick grey face of the opposite end of the cavern. A few feet below me flowed the source of the sound. Crystal clear water. It looked to be only a few feet deep; I could see the white and pink pebbles that lined its bed. Carefully I eased my way down the smooth slope from the tunnel mouth to the creekbed. It seemed warmer here than it had in the tunnel. Hot springs?

I leaned over and dunked my hands into the deceptively still water and confirmed my suspicion. The water was warm, almost bath-warm. I dunked my face to wash off the sweat, and the effect after my exertion was heavenly. All I wanted to do was crawl into a warm tub and relax my aching feet.

And why not? It wasn't as if anyone was going to disturb me here. Setting the flash between two rocks to aim its light to reflect off the wall and onto the water, I stripped off my sweaty clothes and gingerly stepped into the spring water. As I felt the hidden current ripple between my legs, I also felt an embarrassing stirring.

It wasn't as if this were a public pool, I chided myself, and then slid all the way into the water.

I'd been wrong about the depth. My feet couldn't touch the ground unless I dove deep. I soon found myself paddling against the current to remain near my clothes and light, but it was a joyous exertion. I flipped my feet up into the air and slalomed under the water, kicking myself lower and lower until I could grab handfuls of the glittering rock bottom. I soon felt a rash of tickles on my thighs and belly, and had a moment of bladder-voiding fright when I realized there were things in this water with me. What if they were snakes? Poisonous ones?

Trying to control my fright, I eased my way to the bank, all the while feeling the groping of smooth, slippery kisses on my exposed body. I stifled the urge to cry out. At last reaching the light, I directed its beam into the water to discover the source of my discomfort.

They were yellow. About the size of my fist. And apparently, harmless.

Darting in and about my privates were a school of what looked like giant tadpoles. Pale citrus-colored tadpoles with no obvious mouths or eyes. They were flesh with tails.

Keeping hold of the light, I let the current take me again. The creatures followed, bobbing and bumping against my butt and belly. It was a pleasant feeling, their smooth caress, and I found myself relaxing and enjoying their strange attention. In moments I drifted from one end of the cavern to the next, and was faced with the question of whether to duck my head under a rock overhang and follow the stream to its next destination, or to fight the current and go back.

The tadpoles zipped past my legs and disappeared into the under-ledge tunnel. It looked like there might be enough space for my head to surface and breathe between the water and the ceiling, but I opted for safety.

As I climbed out of the water near my clothes, relishing the steamy humidity of the cavern and the tingle of the foreign water dripping from my pores, I knew I would be back. I wanted to see where the stream—and the tadpole creatures—went.

I returned to the underground creek the very next day, better prepared and even more glad to have kept the place secret. I'd felt unusually lustful and amorous after my furtive adventure the day before and had once again tried unsuccessfully to make love to my wife. This time however, it didn't result in quiet fuming, but in a heart-squeezing torrent of bile and bitterness. As we hissed and spat at each other, I could literally feel my love for her distilling into hate.

Later, in the oppressive shadows of the bedroom, I stared at her silken dark hair tangled amidst the sheets. I'd once found it an erotic accoutrement. Now I only longed to yank it, hard, for the feelings its owner had exhumed in my heart. Rolling from the bed, I left the cabin without my clothes, eventually coming to stand naked in a moon-drenched clearing. Despite—or perhaps because of—the bitter fight, I was more aroused as I could ever remember, and sought to still that hunger on my own. As the cool air of the night moved against me in its own secret rhythm, I tried to picture Rachel stretched taut between the pillows of our bed back home. But the only picture that came to mind was of darting, twisting tadpoles.

It was enough.

When I returned to the cave I carried two flashlights and an old oil lamp I'd found tucked away in the cabin's cupboards. This time, I entered the water without hesitation, almost anxiously anticipating the touch of the school of lemon tadpoles. They did not disappoint. Within seconds I felt their nibbles and slickly smooth caresses around my thighs. I'd brought more twine, and sealed my best flash in a ziplock freezer bag to keep it dry. Letting out the rope from where it was anchored near the exit of the watery cavern, I let the current steal me down, down to where the tadpole creatures had passed me the day before. I sucked in a breath and submerged my head beneath the rock ledge. The current was swift, and a pang of fear ripped my gut as I considered the consequences of cracking my head against an outcrop of rock, or of this watery tunnel ending in a sheer waterfall.

My light did little to show me where I was going, its light dissipating before it reached the sides of the sluiceway. I slowed my passage by letting out the twine slower than the current moved. But my need to breathe wouldn't allow me to limit my progress by much. My heart was soon hammering in my head, my lungs screaming for my mouth to open.

And I was through.

My head broke through the water at the same moment as my mouth wrenched itself open to breathe, regardless of my mental instructions not to. I brought up the light as I gasped in the cool fresh air and saw that I was in a cavern similar to the one I'd been in before.

But not quite the same.

At the far end, next to where the river disappeared beneath another shelf of slate, was the most blatantly erotic sculpture I had ever seen. I felt myself growing beneath the water as I stared. It was like the fertility sculptures I'd seen pictures of from ancient cultures. This one was created on an enormous scale. She must have been at least 20 feet tall, and every detail lovingly carved. Rock rivulets of hair cascaded from her forehead to her shoulders and chest. Her lips were heavy and parted, her breasts erect and melonous. But the part that struck me at the start was her sex. She sat at the edge of the water, her legs spread apart, feet submerged. A pile of rocks and mud blocked the current's passage to the open cavern between her thighs, but the original purpose of the V of her stance was obvious.

It wasn't a conscious decision that led to my action. I was suddenly just doing it. Removing the smaller rocks between her calves, digging my fingernails into the packed muck that glued the dam together. Within minutes the water was seeping into crevices that my fingers also worked at. I beat at the stubborn wall using the earliest dislodged stones, and within minutes I was sweating and streaked with black slime. But I was excited. I know now, that feeling must have stemmed from her. With each stone I moved, I felt a surge in my loins, an electric reward. I became a reverse beaver, thrusting against the dam with unexplainable passion, until all at once, the current sloshed over the top of the splintering dam. I lay down on the long-dry tunnel between her legs and with my feet, kicked to loosen the base of the dam. With water pooled on both sides now, it began to give. Then a splash, a slow sucking sound, and the last of the rocks twisted and sunk out of sight. A warm wave passed over my body. As it kissed my face and disappeared into the hole behind my head, I think I had an orgasm.

And then the tickling began.

I hadn't noticed the tadpoles in a while, but the water around me was suddenly thick with them, all surging to dive into the channel I'd just reinvented. I moved out of their way, and the water churned with lemon creatures diving into the statue's sexual abyss. Was this some natural spawning waterway that I had reopened, that some strange artist had commemorated with this statue? I backed up into the central channel again and surveyed my handiwork. The water had risen to kiss the very tops of her thighs, just missed the mark where it would begin dribbling over them. A steady stream of lemon tadpoles disappeared up the tunnel of her exaggerated vagina. None seemed to reappear, and I wondered how far that passage continued into the rock.

I was tired, and felt odd, disconnected, after my exertions so I decided to head back. At first I tried pulling myself along the twine hand over hand, but I soon realized that it was just as easy to swim against the current—it wasn't as strong as it seemed when you just let yourself glide with it. I came up gasping but triumphant in the first cavern, and soon levered myself up on the bank at my backpack. I wolfed down the lunch I'd packed (no Doritos this time) and considered heading home.

The thought of reentering the cabin and sitting across from a sullen Rachel dissuaded that idea quickly. The lunch seemed to instantly restore my strength, and I felt almost an erotic need to plunge into the watery mouth at the opposite end of the pool—to see where the current originated from.

The water was bereft of tads as I kicked my legs and arrowed under a new ledge. Again the light failed to show my way, but I wasn't worried this time. I was unlikely to swim my way into a rock hard enough to knock myself out, and I surely wasn't going to go over a fall with water rushing opposite my chosen course.

This tunnel seemed shorter than the southern passage, and within seconds I popped my head up in a new pool, in a new cavern.

This was the place I'd searched for.

I shone my light on the walls and laughed out loud.

"Holy shit," I said to no one.

The place was beautiful. And a mouth of rocky teeth. Stretching many feet from the ceiling were tiers of blue-green and blushing stalactites, and rising from the floor on the sides of the pool were an equally dizzying number of multicolored stalagmites. It was like swimming in the midst of a shark's mouth.

I swam to a bank and ran my hand up and down one of the glossy rock needles. It was smooth and cool. Like a marble column shellacked in varnish. I longed to break it off, but didn't want to mar the beauty of the place by destruction. Perhaps I could find one that had fallen from the roof?

I climbed the bank and walked gingerly along the shore, uncomfortably aware of the consequences if I slipped on the smooth stone floor and landed heavily on the points of the stone spears that were everywhere around me. I stared at the path carefully, catching sight occasionally of a darting tadpole speeding towards the entry tunnel.

At last, I came to the last turn of the cavern. I'd found no broken spears, but I nearly slipped and ate one when I saw the guardian to the end of this chamber.

A man to match the woman.

He was gargantuan, like her, and in the same posture: back to the wall, legs spread to capture the water. But there was no blockage to prevent his giant sex organ from hanging into the current. Hanging, actually is incorrect. He seemed in a state of excitement, if the sculptor was attempting to work to scale. (It's hard to tell really—should a 20 foot man have a three foot organ, or only a foot and a half? His was at least arm's length).

I slid back in the water, and swam to the icon's feet. Its chest was bulging, shadowed muscle, its arms were clasped behind its head. Eyes closed, it seemed wholly at peace as it let its lower body dangle in the water.

But it wasn't at peace. It was in my head.

"Bring her to me," I heard clearly, though not with my ears. Its face remained passive, but I swear to God it spoke to me, threatened me. A vision flashed in my mind of what it wanted as it spoke.

"Bring her or meet my children."

In my mind I caught a glimpse of a pulsing mountain of flesh, warted gleaming gold eyes, and teeth. Teeth everywhere. A crash came from my left. A stalactite had somehow dislodged from the ceiling to land a yard from where I stood.

"Promise to bring her, or the next one will not miss. Use it. Bring her."

I promised. Then I grabbed the stone spear and dove back into the current. I almost forgot to pull my pants and backpack back on before running down the long slope out of the mountain.

"You have to come see this cavern," I crowed that night. Rachel looked at me with something less than boredom.

"I've never liked caves," she sighed. "And I don't think I like you anymore, either. So why would I want to go to a cave with you?"

"It'll be quick, I promise. Just humor me one more time, OK?"

"And I'll get what out of it? Claustrophobic and clammy? No thanks."

But I didn't let up. Finally she gave in, simply, I think, to shut me up. Reasons didn't matter. I smiled inwardly. And as we lay down to another sexless night, I dreamed of nuzzling citrus tadpoles and an amazon stone woman. The sheets were sticky when I woke in a warm sweat to the sound of croaking frogs.

Rachel complained the entire walk up the inside of the mountain, which only strengthened my resolve. The closer I got to the cavern, the less I heard of her. My mind began remembering the sensation of the tadpoles against my legs, of the watery extended orgasm I'd experienced in opening a channel to the statue woman's deep and thirsty tunnel. And I remembered the vision of her partner.

When we reached the cavern, Rachel looked around with her flashlight. Her face dropped. "Where are the stalagmites?"

I was already peeling off my clothes.

"We have to swim for them."

"I'm not diving into that! You don't know what things are in there. Caves have all sorts of weird fish and things with no eyes swimming around in them. Uh. Uh."

"I've been in a couple times now," I said. "It's fine."

She turned her back to me and began to retrace our steps.

"Goodbye, Jim. I'm going to the cabin, packing, and leaving. You stay here in your little cave."

I threw myself at her, my shoulders connecting with the backs of her knees. She fell hard, crying out as her head cracked against the rock floor. The force knocked her out, and something inside me whispered "it's easier this way."

I pulled her back into the cavern, and saw the swelling on her forehead already goosehead big and blue. She was breathing fine, so I undressed her and pulled her into the water with me. Immediately a swarm of tadpoles gathered around us, but this time they concentrated, not on mine, but on Rachel's thighs. She moaned slightly, and I swam to the giant man's tunnel quickly, before she came to completely. I held her with one arm around her chest, and felt myself swelling at the feel of her familiar yet still tantalizing breasts. I pulled her under the water with me, and the dunking served to wake her fully. She started clawing at me, but I only gripped her harder, and pushed us against the current the short space underwater until we could surface in the stalagmite cavern.

I let her go when we broke the surface, and she immediately dove away from me, choking and crying at the same time.

"You're crazy," she yelled, and swam ahead as I chased her.

Chased her right to the statue.

She was as awed as I had been.

For a moment, she seemed to forget my coercion, as she rose from the water to stand at the feet of the giant. My flash played upon her dripping buttocks, and I was suddenly overcome. I believe it was the giant and not myself. But something happened to her too. Because when I walked up behind her and reached my hands around her waist to feel her up, she didn't push me away. And when I ran those same hands down the trail of her belly, into the light down of her pubes, she changed her stance to accommodate.

When I turned her to face me, she had a blank, lost look in her eyes. Concussion or possession, I don't know, but without any suggestion from me, she suddenly knelt and put her mouth to work. Something she'd never done for me. Ever.

I was in ecstasy, but she wasn't finished. Smiling a retarded sort of grin, she stepped into the water between the giant's legs, and got down on her hands and knees. Only her hands were clutching the giant's phallus, and her rear was waving in a gesture that not many men could ignore under any circumstance.

I took my wife for the last time there, in a cave, her hands on another's organ. A rod of stone. And as I found the best release I can ever remember having, a swarm of golden tadpoles shot from the rock between my wife's hands and darted around us slickly kissing our every pore. I almost loved her again in that moment.

And then the spell wore off.

And she screamed.

"Oh my God, what have you done!"

The tads were not letting up this time, and Rachel soon showed me why.

"I can't move my hands!" she wailed, and holding her arms up, I saw they were entwined together with hundreds of tiny lemon filaments.

In that instant, I saw again the vision I'd seen before, and again a rocky spear fell nearby to remind me of my promise.

"Come on," I said and tugged her back into the channel. "Let the current take us back."

In seconds we'd resurfaced in the main cavern. I heard it then.

The heavy thunder that rose above the sound of the gurgling river. It came from her cavern. It sounded like the croaking of a thousand bullfrogs. And as we swam to the shore, it grew louder.

I pulled her out of the water, and then reached down to pick up the twine I'd used to mark my progress. Before she knew what I intended, I looped the twine through her glued hands, and tied her fast. She could move to the water's edge and stand in the lip of the exit, but could go no farther.

"What are you doing? You can't mean to leave me here!"

I looked into her face, and tried to remember why I had once loved her. Instead a strange sensation rumbled through my stomach.

Hunger.

Insatiable, painful hunger. It grew with the sound of the now not-so-distant croaking.

"I do," I said, and like the last life-changing time I'd said it to her, I really did mean it.

Something huge and glisteningly green broke the surface of the water as I turned from her and ran to the exit.

I forgot my clothes this time, but it didn't matter anymore, did it?

I'm all packed now, and ready to leave. I want so badly to walk up that trail once more, and bathe in the waters of the lusty cavern. But I don't know if Rachel only bought me time, or bought me endless license. If the former, my meter is up. Last night as I lay alone in bed, my belly rumbled contentedly, as my sheets became stained with uninitiated pleasure.

This morning I stood at the base of the mountain, in the dry streambed where I'd first discovered the hidden tunnel. The otherwise white stones were marred in spots with something sticky. Something dusky red. A shred of the t-shirt I'd ripped off Rachel was caught in a bush nearby. And every few feet, glistening and shriveling in the sun, were thin, sticky threads.

Yellow threads. Like cornsilk.

As I stood there contemplating the evidence of my betrayal, I felt a rumbling in my stomach. And a stirring in my loins. Suddenly I wanted to rip off my clothes, run up the hidden tunnel and plunge into the secret pool again.

But I didn't.

Sometimes being a coward has its advantages. It helped me run.

But can I stay away?

And if so, can they follow me?

As I turn the car onto the first paved road in 20 miles, I can swear I hear croaking behind me. Not too far away. And not diminishing.

I feel hungry.

ABOUT THE AUTHOR

John Everson is the Bram Stoker Award-winning author of the novels *Covenant*, *Sacrifice*, *The 13th* and *Siren*, and the short story collections *Deadly Nightlusts*, *Creeptych*, *Needles & Sins*, *Vigilantes of Love* and *Cage of Bones & Other Deadly Obsessions*.

John shares a deep purple den in Naperville, Illinois with a cockatoo and cockatiel, a disparate collection of fake skulls, twisted skeletal fairies, Alan Clark illustrations and a large stuffed Eeyore. There's also a mounted Chinese fowling spider named Stoker courtesy of Charlee Jacob, an ever-growing shelf of custom mix CDs and an acoustic guitar that he can't really play but that his son Shaun likes to hear him beat on anyway. Sometimes his wife Geri is surprised to find him shuffling through more public areas of the house, but it's usually only to brew another cup of coffee. In order to avoid the onerous task of writing, he holds down a regular job at a medical association, records pop-rock songs in a hidden home studio, experiments with the insatiable culinary joys of the jalapeno, designs photo collage art book covers for a variety of small presses, loses hours in expanding an array of gardens and chases frequent excursions into the bizarre visual headspace of '70s euro-horror DVDs with a shot of Makers Mark and a tall glass of Newcastle.

For information on his fiction, art and music, visit John Everson: Dark Arts at www.johneverson.com.

Dark Quest Books Brings You
More Dark and Disturbing Fiction

IN A GILDED LIGHT
Jennifer Brozek
9780982619766

BEAUTY HAS HER WAY
Jennifer Brozek
9780983099314

DARK FUTURES
Jason Sizemore
9780982619728

SOUL BORN
Kevin James Breaux
9780983099321

IN AN IRON CAGE
Danielle Ackley-McPhail
and Neal Levin
9780982619742

The Evil Gazebo
Bernie Mojzes
9780974664569

Shimmer
Jonathan Passarella
9780974664576

...and Other Great Titles from Dark Quest Books

BREACH THE HULL
9780979690198
SO IT BEGINS
9780979690150
BY OTHER MEANS
9780983099352
Mike McPhail

DRAGON'S LURE
Danielle Ackley-McPhail
9780982619797

THE HALFING'S COURT
Danielle Ackley-McPhail
9780979690167

WHERE ANGELS FEAR
CJ Henderson
and
Bruce Gewheller
9780982619711

THE LITERARY HANDYMAN
Danielle Ackley-McPhail
(Forthcoming)

Please see our website for further details www.darkquestbooks.com

The books that put the Dark into Dark Quest...

MYSTIC INVESTIGATORS:
9780979690143
BULLETS AND BRIMSTONE
9780982619735
and
FROM THE SHADOWS
Patrick Thomas
(Forthcoming)

DEAR CTHULHU:
HAVE A DARK DAY
9780979690137
and
GOOD ADVICE
FOR BAD PEOPLE
9780982619742
Patrick Thomas

HERE THERE BE MONSTERS
John L. French
9780982619773